# The Price

## *of*

# Honor

# OTHER BOOKS

# The Price

*of*

# Honor

Dragon Riders of Osnen Prequels
Book 1

RICHARD FIERCE

The Price of Honor
Copyright © 2022 by Richard Fierce

Cover design by germancreative
Cover art by David Gaillet

Dragonfire Press

e-Book ISBN: 978-1-947329-95-9

Print ISBN: 978-1-947329-96-6

First Edition: 2022

Let your plans be dark and impenetrable as night, and when you move, fall like a thunderbolt.

-Sun Tzu

L AILANI WALKED BAREFOOT across the sand, watching the waves crash upon the shore. She loved the sound the water made. It was soothing, peaceful. Grit gathered between her toes, but she didn't mind. It wasn't often that she could go without shoes, and she enjoyed the moment of freedom.

Ahead, a jagged rock formation protruded up from the smooth sand, revealing a sea cave. The waves lapped at its base, feeding a small pool. Lailani paused to look at the water, judging the level of the tide. It was low, which was what she'd hoped for. The sky was clear, and the sun shone brightly on the water's surface.

It was a beautiful day for a ride.

Lailani stepped through the pool and looked into the dark entrance of the cave that was carved into the rock. She didn't know how long it had existed on the island, but she knew Daigo was glad it did. He'd called it home for as long as she'd been alive. She entered the cave and picked up a loose stone from the floor, then tapped it against the wall.

The sound echoed into the darkness until it eventually faded. She waited for a moment, then repeated the tapping. Daigo stirred in the darkness. She could hear his wings stretching and the scrape of his talons on the stone floor as he approached.

*You're late.*

His words resonated within her mind.

*Sorry,* she replied. *I had to finish my chores first.*

Daigo was her father's dragon, but she spent the most time with him. Her father's arthritis had debilitated him, and since he could no longer ride, she took it upon herself to ensure the dragon left his cave each day.

*Completing your duties is important. It teaches responsibility.*

*That's what father always says.*

*You would do well to take his lessons to heart. He's a wise man.*

*Doesn't your name mean wise?*

Daigo chortled. *It means enlightenment, but close enough.*

They walked side by side, away from the cave and onto the beach. Daigo's massive claws left deep impressions in the sand, and they quickly filled with water. His scales were a vibrant cobalt hue, and when the light hit them at just the right angle, they seemed to glow with fluorescent rainbows. She hadn't seen many dragons in her short lifespan, but she believed he was the most regal of them all.

Lailani often dreamed of becoming a Dragon Guard, but it was forbidden to her. It wasn't her father that forbade her, but the law of the land. Only men could bond with dragons. She didn't think it was fair, but as long as she had Daigo's companionship, she was happy. While dragons could only bond with one person, they could communicate with any human they chose, and Lailani counted it a great honor that Daigo allowed her to ride on his back, let alone speak to her.

*Where should we fly today?*

*I was thinking about that before you arrived, and I know just the place.*

Lailani waited for him to continue, but he said nothing.

*Well?*

*Patience, small one. Climb on and I'll show you. It's a surprise.*

A grin spread across her lips as she grabbed onto his shoulder and climbed up onto his back. She sat between his shoulder blades and pressed her knees tightly against the base of his neck.

*I'm ready.*

Daigo lowered himself like a cat about to pounce, then leaped into the air. He flapped his powerful wings, lifting them steadily higher until they were soaring over the Sea of Colisle. Lailani looked back and saw the shore growing smaller. They lived on the Perched Cay, just one of a few islands that were clustered together several miles from the mainland. She could see them all from her vantage point, and the view was breathtaking.

Lailani turned her attention forward and tried to guess where Daigo was taking her. She spotted a thick mist hanging over the water below.

*What's that?* she asked.

*The Mists of Mourning. Never go there.*

*Why not?*

*It is where the dead go to find rest.*

Lailani shrank back, tracing a warding symbol in the air. She wanted nothing to do with the spirits of the dead. They flew along the mist line and continued further out to sea. There was nothing but water in every direction, and it stretched as far as she could see.

*I think this is the farthest I've been from home.*

*How does that make you feel?* Daigo asked.

*I'm not sure. I like seeing new places, but there's something comforting about the familiar.*

*You have lived your entire life on the Perched Cay, but it is only a sliver of the world. There are a great many things to see outside of the island. Your father and I used to travel all over the mainland.*

*What was it like?*

*If we were bonded, I could show you my memories and let you experience them for yourself. Alas, words will have to do. Those days were good.*

*We had many adventures and fought many enemies together.*

*My father's sword rests beside the hearth in our house.*

*And his armor?*

*He keeps it in his room, though I doubt he could still fit into it. I think he used to be smaller back then.*

*He was,* Daigo said. *Time and food tend to make humans plump.*

Lailani giggled in response. They spent hours gliding over the sea, and Daigo related stories of her father's days at the Terranese school, including how the two of them had met. She knew the story of how her father had bonded with Daigo, but it never grew old no matter how many times she heard it. They were heading home as he related the tale, and she listened intently despite knowing it so well.

*Your father was a quiet man. He joined the school to learn the ways of war so that he could earn the money needed to take care of his parents. They suffered from the same illness that he has now, and they weren't able to harvest their crops. He was strong and stubborn, and once he was admitted as a student, he had trouble matching with a dragon.*

*Until he found you,* Lailani said.

*Yes. I saw past his rough exterior and knew that bonding with him would be good for both of us. He was about to be forced from the school when I offered to bond with him. He agreed, and over time, he proved me right.*

*That he wasn't so rough?*

*Indeed. He may seem that way, but deep down, he has a soft heart.*

She knew that was true. Her father often went out of his way to help others in need, even if it meant he would go without. As the Perched Cay came into view, Lailani spotted a group of dark clouds traveling swiftly across the sky.

*Do you see that?* she asked.

*I see them.*

*Them?*

*Dragons with their riders. Five of them.*

Excitement flashed through her. She leaned forward, squinting to make out their details. They were still too far away, but she saw they were descending. They broke formation, and each dragon wheeled down toward a different island.

*What do you suppose they are doing?*

*We shall find out soon enough.*

Daigo began his own descent to the island, and they landed gently on the beach. Lailani leaped off the dragon's back and sprinted across the sand, stopping momentarily to wave at the dragon.

*Thank you for the flight! I'll let you know what I find out!*

*Very good, little one.*

She ran as fast as she could, weaving between trees and rocks, excitement driving her onward even as her lungs burned within her chest. The jungle opened up to a large flat field where the town was located. The dragon she'd seen was on the outskirts, but she noticed a crowd had gathered in the center of town.

Her father was there, as were her friends Kalea and Huou. She joined the two men. They smiled at her, sharing her excitement at the visitor.

"What did I miss?" Lailani asked.

"Nothing. He just got here."

Lailani peered through the press of bodies and got a glimpse of the rider. He was wearing a full suit of armor, his helmet tucked under his arm. The mask of the helmet was painted with a demonic face, its eyes burning with anger. His black boots gleamed with fresh polish, and a sword was strapped to his waist. The man's air of importance intrigued Lailani.

"Citizens of the Perched Cay, I come bearing a message from the emperor!"

Conversations died, and the man swept his gaze across the crowd.

"War is coming. The Roarans have crossed the border, killing and destroying all in their path. The emperor is calling all retired riders back into service, effective immediately. You will have the rest of the day to settle your affairs, and you are to report to the school in the morning. If you are unfit for battle, you must send your son in your place. If you do not have a son, then you will report regardless."

Lailani's heart dropped into her stomach. Her father couldn't fight. He could barely walk most days. And she was his only child. A lump formed in her throat and she looked at her friends. Their expressions were serious.

"What will my father do?" she asked. "He can't go to war."

"Neither can ours," Huou said.

"Looks like we'll be going in their place," Kalea added, sharing a look with Huou.

Her father and Daigo were all the family she had. If they were gone, she would have nobody, especially if her friends had to leave. There had to be another option, a way to keep her father from going.

Lailani's world was crashing around her.

A S THE SUN began its descent beyond the horizon, Lailani sat at the table, absently picking at her plate of food. Her father had cooked lavishly compared to their typical fare, probably to cheer her up, but she wasn't hungry. He had spoken little since they'd come home, and the silence stretched between them even now.

She was angry and scared. Angry because her father had already done his duty, and scared because she didn't know what she would do if she lost him. Lailani could feel her father's eyes on her, and she met his gaze.

"I know you have something to say, so speak your mind."

"You can't go," she said.

"I have to."

"Why? You can't ride anymore. What good will it do for them to have you there? You already served the empire and did your duty."

"It is a matter of honor, Lailani."

"Honor means nothing if you are dead."

"Perhaps, but I will die knowing that I kept you safe."

"I'm not a child anymore. I don't need you to protect me from invaders on the mainland."

Her father sighed, and she immediately felt guilty.

"I'm sorry. I didn't mean …" She trailed off, trying to find the right words, but her emotions made it difficult. "There are plenty of men willing to fight. Let them go."

"You have every right to feel the way you do. I don't fault you for it, but I *am* going. You are right, Lailani. You are not a child anymore. Your mother would be proud of you."

Her eyes welled with tears at the mention of her mother. Although it had been three years since her death, the grief still stung her heart as if she had passed into eternity yesterday.

"I am going to bed," her father said, rising from his chair.

He slowly made his way to his room, leaving Lailani to clear the table. She did so sullenly, her mind refusing to accept that her father would be leaving tomorrow. Daigo would go with him, and then she would be alone. The tears fell down her cheeks now, and she didn't bother to wipe them away.

Once Lailani finished cleaning, she went to the shrine outside of their home and placed the portion of food her father had prepared for their ancestors on the altar and knelt before it, praying for guidance. As usual, they did not reply to her.

Rising to her feet, she went back into the house and stood in front of the hearth. The flames burned low, casting flickering shadows on the edges of her vision. The blade of her father's sword glinted, and she turned her gaze on it. Its pommel held a large sapphire stone and the grip was wrapped in black leather. The crossbar was straight and unadorned, but the blade made up for the lack of decoration. Engraved on the surface of the metal were graceful wingless dragons.

Lailani had always viewed the weapon as a thing of beauty. She couldn't believe her father had wielded it in countless battles, that it had taken the lives of so many people. She clenched her jaw. If the empire forced her father to wield it again, she had no doubt he would die. Her throat constricted, and she covered her mouth with her hand, fearing that she would wake her father with her anguish.

If only she had a brother, or had been born a boy, then she would willingly go in his place. Her father deserved to enjoy the rest of his days in peace, not die in battle as a crippled old man, but she knew better than anyone how stubborn he was. He would answer the emperor's call because his honor demanded it, ignoring any logical arguments against the decision.

Lailani grabbed the sword from the rack and held it up, looking at her reflection in the blade. Everyone always said she looked like her mother, but she didn't see it. When she looked at herself, she saw her father more than anything. Black hair, olive skin, hooded deep-set green eyes, the angular form of her face ... there was no mistaking her lineage. If her hair was shorter, she could almost pass as a son.

She sucked in a breath.

It was foolish, insane even. She couldn't ... could she? Without a second thought, she tilted her head and ran her fingers through her hair, clasping tightly to the ends. Holding the edge of the blade against her hair, she stood unmoving for a moment. If she did this, there was no turning back. And if they caught her, she would be executed. But it was worth the risk if she could spare her father.

With a single move, Lailani cut her hair.

She held the strands briefly before releasing them. They dropped to the floor, and her eyes widened. It was too late to stop now. She cut the rest of it and tossed the loose hair into the hearth. Her father would be upset with her when he found out, but she had to do it. She left the sword on the table and quietly slipped into her father's room.

His breathing was steady, and in between every few breaths, a soft snore escaped him. Lailani stepped lightly to his bedside and smiled as she stared at him. Although the room was dark, a small flickering candle on the side table illuminated his face. His normally wrinkled visage was smooth, his worries temporarily erased.

"Sleep well," she whispered. "And forgive me."

Her father's armor lay on his desk, and the faint scent of rapeseed oil drifted in the air. She carefully retrieved each piece and snuck them out of the room, then stuffed them into a sack and slung it over her shoulder. She wrapped the scabbard belt around her waist and retrieved the sword, sheathing it, and grabbed the parchment with his summons.

Lailani cast one last look around the room and steeled her emotions. She didn't know if she'd ever come back home, if she'd ever see her father again. The temptation to stay was strong, but she knew this was the only way to save him. She left, fleeing into the night, her steps leading her to Daigo's cave.

Waves lapped at the shore, and the shadowy outlines of crabs scuttling across the sand caught her attention. She slowed her pace as the cave's entrance came into view. This was going to be the trickiest part of her plan. If Daigo refused to help her, it would all fall apart. She rehearsed her argument within her mind as she walked, preparing to debate with the dragon.

Lailani stepped into the cave and felt around blindly for a rock. Her fingers grazed one, and she lifted it, tapping it against the wall as she had earlier.

*Little one,* Daigo greeted. *What are you doing here so late?*

*I came to tell you about the dragon rider. Did I wake you?*

*No. I'm having difficulty sleeping. Something must trouble your father. The bond is filled with his anxiety.*

Lailani frowned. *It's because of what the rider said.*

*What did he say?*

*Father didn't tell you?*

*I'm afraid not,* Daigo said. *He normally keeps his end of the bond sealed shut.*

Lailani found that curious. *The rider was a messenger. War is coming, and the emperor has issued a decree requiring all dragon riders to return to the school.*

*You jest.*

*I'm not,* Lailani replied. *Though I wish I was. You know as well as I that father cannot go. His illness will be his death.*

Daigo growled, the sound echoing along the cave walls.

*Your father retired.*

*The emperor doesn't care about that. If he doesn't go, he'll be imprisoned.*

*That fate is better than death.*

*Maybe, but you know father won't shirk his responsibilities. He plans to leave in the morning. I tried talking him out of it, but he's stubborn.*

*I know well how hard his head can be. If he goes, then so must I. We aren't just bonded. We swore an oath to protect one another.*

*What if someone else went in his place? Would you go with them instead?*

*Who do you speak of?*

*It's just a question,* Lailani said.

*Without a bond, it would be difficult.*

*We're not bonded, yet we can communicate.*

*Yes, but I cannot see your memories or hear your thoughts. There is a difference between speaking with one another and sharing a bond. Allowing someone else to be my rider would not be ideal, especially if I don't know them.*

*What if you did know them?*

*It would still be difficult. Let me come out to the beach and we can talk under the stars.*

Lailani left the cave and waited for the dragon. Daigo soon joined her and he stretched his wings. He craned his head up to look at the stars, then turned his gaze on her.

*You cut your hair,* he said. His eyes narrowed. *And you carry a pack that stinks of leather and oil. Explain yourself.*

Lailani inhaled a deep breath.

*I'm going in my father's place, and I need you to take me.*

SILENCE STRETCHED BETWEEN them, and Lailani feared he would refuse.

*I can't let father go. He'll die, and I can't allow that. You said you swore an oath to protect him. If you want to honor that oath, then you'll take me instead.*

Daigo stared at her intensely. She could hear the waves lapping at the shore and the nighttime sounds of the animals on the island, but they were only faint background noise. Lailani's sole focus was on willing Daigo to say yes.

After what felt like an eternity, the dragon looked up at the sky again and issued a rumble from deep within his chest.

*It will not be easy.*

*I know.*

*It will be dangerous.*

*This I also know.*

*If they find out you are a woman ...*

*I'll die,* Lailani said. *I'm aware of the risks. I've considered them a hundred times as I walked here.*

*You are stubborn like your father. Perhaps that will be helpful. If I take you, you must promise me something.*

*Anything. What is it?*

*If they discover your true identity, you must kill me.*

*What?* She scrunched her face in surprise.

*If I dishonor the empire, they will put me to death as well. It will be mercilessly. I do not want to die like that. You must strike me in the heart with your blade. I want a warrior's death.*

Lailani's throat rapidly swelled, and she had trouble speaking. She coughed harshly and placed her hand over her heart.

*I will do as you ask.*

*It didn't take you long to make that decision.*

*I don't plan on being discovered, so neither of us will have to worry about that.*

Daigo turned back to her and exhaled through his nose, his warm breath ruffling her hair.

*You brought armor and weapons but forgot the saddle.*

*I couldn't carry it all. I'll leave the pack here and go get it.*

*Be quick or I'll change my mind.*

Lailani turned and sprinted across the beach, the moon providing plenty of light to see by. She raced all the way home and hurried into the small shack her father had built many years ago. The saddle was on a sawhorse table, and the scent of fresh oil hit her nostrils. Her father had prepared everything. Lailani retrieved it and hefted it over her shoulder, then stepped back into the night.

Voices drifted in the air, and she froze in place. She cocked her head to the side, listening. It was Kalea and his father. Their house was a stone's throw from hers, separated only by shrubbery, and Lailani snuck closer to listen to what they were talking about.

"It will take some time for you to get used to your dragon," Makani, Kalea's father, said. "Do not be impatient. That will only make things worse."

"Yes, father."

"There are many colors, but pray you do not bond with a black dragon. They are conniving creatures, and do not obey orders very well."

"I hope to bond with a blue dragon," Kalea said. "Just imagine the look on an enemy's face when they see a bolt of lightning coming straight at them."

Makani *tsked*. "You won't think it's very exciting when you see the death and destruction a dragon can cause. Some people never recover from the trauma they experience."

"I'm not excited, father. I'm scared. Jokes ease the fear a little."

Makani placed a hand on Kalea's shoulder, his expression serious. "I would be worried if you weren't afraid. War is ugly, and only the mentally disturbed enjoy killing others."

"Please tell me everything is going to be fine. I know that it's not going to be, but for some reason, I feel as though it will be if you say so."

Lailani's eyes welled with tears. Everything was happening so quickly, but now that she had a moment to think about it, she was terrified. The uncertainty and risks were an invisible weight, heavier than the saddle upon her shoulder, but she knew that none of that ultimately mattered. So long as she kept her father from going to war, she would face sword and flame willingly.

Makani and Kalea went inside their home, and Lailani grunted under the heft of the saddle. She turned and left, heading back to the beach where Daigo was waiting for her. The dragon lowered himself to the ground and she set the saddle in place, then ducked under him as he rose and connected the straps across his chest.

*Is that too tight?*

*It's too loose. Tighten the center straps.*

Lailani did so, using all of her strength to pull the strap as taut as possible. She forced the metal prongs through the punch holes and checked the other straps. They were all snug.

*Better?*

*Yes. Are you sure you want to do this?* Daigo asked. *There is no turning back once we get there.*

His question gave her pause. Was she ready? This was her last chance to change her mind. She thought about her father and it gave her strength.

*I'm sure.*

*Then climb on, little one. We go to war.*

She stepped out from under him and he bent his legs, sinking low. Lailani grabbed the bag with the armor, strapping it securely to the saddle, then grabbed ahold of the saddle horn and placed her left foot in the stirrup. With a hop, she pulled herself up and swung her right leg up and over, landing squarely in the saddle. She positioned her right foot into the other stirrup and squeezed her knees tight against him.

Daigo didn't wait for her to say she was ready. He leaped into the air and flapped his wings, gaining altitude over the water before turning east. Lailani had never been to the mainland before. She had only seen it from afar, and only when she was on the far side of the island, a place she rarely visited. Her palms were sweaty, and they kept slipping free of the saddle horn despite the many times she wiped them on her gown.

She watched the dark water below as they flew, trying to keep her mind occupied. It was no use. Her thoughts ran wild with fearful images of her and Daigo being killed in the most brutal fashions. She was glad at that moment that she couldn't share her thoughts with the dragon. He probably would have turned around and taken her home.

Within a few hours, they crossed the sea and left the coast behind. Daigo adjusted their course to the north, and after another half hour, the encampment outside of the school came into view. The wind picked up, making the thousands of fires that dotted the landscape below flicker. The sight reminded Lailani of fireflies, and she smiled, her fear briefly forgotten.

*You will need to change clothes before you report in,* Daigo said.

Lailani's eyes widened. She had brought none of her father's clothes with her. Not that she could have, since they wouldn't have fit her, anyway.

*The only thing I have is the gown I'm wearing.*

*You can't show up wearing that. They'll never believe you're a man.*

*I guess I didn't think that far ahead. What do we do now?*

Daigo began descending and turned away from the encampment.

*You will need to find some clothes. A single pair will do. You can always wash them if you have time.*

The idea of marching around in dirty clothes wasn't appealing, but she knew he was right. One pair of clothes was better than nothing. Daigo landed gently in a field of tall grass a fair distance from the camp, and Lailani dismounted.

*You're not likely to find anything at the school even if they let you inside, so you'll need to find something from the camp.*

*I don't have any money,* Lailani said.

*Then you must steal what you need.*

*Steal?* The word was as foreign to her as the mainland. *I've never stolen anything in my life.*

*There is a first time for everything,* Daigo replied. *You will do many things you are not proud of. At least the foremost one isn't murder.*

*I don't even know who you are right now.*

*You aren't on the island anymore, little one. The wide world is a place full of cruelty and power-hungry people. The quicker your eyes are open to these truths, the better off you'll be.*

Lailani realized that she'd gotten herself into much more than she bargained for. Everyone on the island was friendly. The only exception was Merrick. He was from the mainland and moved to the island a few years ago, but he wasn't cruel. He was just an old grump. If the world was full of people meaner than him, she wasn't sure how she was going to handle it.

*I'll wait here for you. And don't get caught. The penalty for theft is the loss of a hand.*

*That's great,* she said sarcastically.

Lailani turned toward the camp and started walking.

4

A S LAILANI SNUCK along the shadows between the tents, she was thankful they had arrived under the cover of darkness. It made it easier for her to hide, but it also allowed her to get a glimpse of the camp before she officially took her place among the other riders.

Boisterous laughter and voices raised in conversation mingled in the night air, and she used the loud sounds to her advantage, jogging instead of creeping when she could. Her plan had been to get some clothes and quickly get out, but it was becoming clear that would not happen. All the tents she passed had occupants, and the longer she was there, the more her chances of being caught increased.

The long row of tents abruptly ended, and Lailani paused. An enormous purple pavilion stood alone, towering three times as high as the other tents, which all seemed so plain in comparison. A lone soldier guarded the entrance, but unlike the other tents, there was no light shining inside this one. She decided it was the ideal target, and she hurried across the clearing to the back side of the tent. The guard didn't notice her, and she wasn't entirely sure that he was even awake.

Lailani glanced around, then lifted the bottom edge of the tent and slipped underneath. A plush rug covered the ground, providing a comfortable makeshift floor. A candle burned on a silver tray atop a desk near her, and she grabbed it. Holding it up high, she spotted an ornate chest with dragon engravings. It rested at the foot of an enormous bed, and she rushed over to it and opened the lid.

An assortment of tunics and trousers were inside, perfectly folded into neat piles. She balanced the candle on the edge of the chest and pulled a tunic out and held it up to herself. It looked like it would fit her, so she slung it over her shoulder and grabbed a matching pair of trousers. They also looked like they would fit, so she took those as well and returned the candle to the desk. Judging by all the expensive items, Lailani assumed that whoever owned the tent must be important.

She slipped out into the night and navigated back the way she'd come. Halfway along the row of tents, she realized she didn't grab any boots. She couldn't wear her woven straw sandals. They were practically falling apart, anyway. Lailani turned around and headed back toward the large tent, but when she reached the clearing, she saw a ring of guards had surrounded it.

They all stood relaxed, and Lailani breathed a sigh of relief. It didn't appear anyone knew she'd been inside. She wouldn't be able to get boots from there, so she would have to find them from another tent. That meant she would have to steal from two people instead of one. She groaned. Her father had told her stories of his battles, but he had never really talked about much else. Had he been forced to steal from other people as well?

Lailani turned around yet again and listened to the voices inside the tents as she walked. It was late, but these people didn't seem to care. She happened upon a tent that was dark, and when she rested her ear against the canvas, she heard light snoring. Excitement welled within her and she tried to lift the bottom of the tent as she had at the pavilion, but the material was cinched tightly over the tent poles.

Frowning, Lailani slowly circled around to the entrance. She cautiously swept her gaze up and down the row. It was empty. She peeked her head inside the tent and spotted a dirty pair of boots sitting on the floor. Lailani grabbed them and hurried back into the shadows, then made her way out into the field where Daigo waited. She paused behind him and quickly changed clothes, rolling her gown into a ball, then slipped the boots on and cursed under her breath when she realized they were too big. She stomped on the ground a few times, and Daigo turned to look at her.

*You almost look like a man.*

*Almost?*

*Your face is too soft and pretty.*

*So this will not work?*

*I didn't say that,* Daigo replied. *I'm saying that you are a pretty man. The other riders may not take to you very well.*

*I don't care what they think.*

*There's your father's stubbornness. Don't lose that trait. It will do you well. Perhaps you should rub some dirt on your face to hide your beauty.*

Lailani scowled, but she knew Daigo wouldn't lead her astray. She knelt in the grass and dug her hands into the soil, then rubbed her fingers over her face. Being dirty wasn't something she was a stranger to, but she didn't think her first impression with the other riders would be ideal. When she turned to face the camp, a wave of intense fear washed over her.

*Do we have to report in tonight?* She looked at Daigo pleadingly, but said nothing else.

*We can wait until morning,* he replied. *That means we'll have to sleep under the stars.*

*I'm fine with that. It'll be like when you and I slept on the beach.*

Daigo chuckled, the sound deep and baritone.

*Those are fond memories, though your father always got upset because he thought you'd run off somewhere.*

Lailani smiled, remembering the many stern reprimands he'd given her. Still, she always wound up on the beach with Daigo, watching the stars and listening to him tell stories of his travels with her father until the early morning hours. That was when her mother was still alive. Her smile faded.

*Should we sleep here?*

*Probably not. The woods behind the school will provide some shelter, and I smell rain on the wind.*

*A storm?*

*Nothing strong, unless my nose deceives me.*

Daigo had never been wrong about the weather before. She climbed into the saddle and he leaped into the air, flying over the school's gracefully curved roofs. He landed in a clearing among the tall trees and she dismounted. The woods were silent at first, and then crickets chirped their nighttime songs. Lailani retrieved her bag and unstrapped the saddle, and Daigo curled up beneath an enormous tree.

*This spot should do well,* he said.

*Should one of us stay up to make sure nothing happens?*

*What would happen?*

*I don't know. If the Roarans have invaded Terran, how do we know they aren't here?*

*The school is the heart of our strength. If the Roarans had gotten this far, the school wouldn't be standing and there wouldn't be an army camped outside of it. We are safe, little one.*

His words eased Lailani's worries, and she walked over and sat on the ground, leaning back against him and using her rolled-up gown as a pillow. She was tired, exhausted even, and dawn wasn't far off. If she fell asleep now, she could still get a few hours of rest. It was better than nothing. She closed her eyes and drifted off into darkness.

It seemed as if she had just nodded off when her eyes opened. She stared up at the canopy. The wind rustled among the foliage, but that wasn't what had woken her. It was something else, something … her tired mind told her to go back to sleep. Her eyelids drooped, and then she sat upright as a bright flash of lightning lit up the sky. A moment later, thunder echoed across the landscape.

Lailani's heart pounded in her chest. Her brain was foggy, still being half asleep, and she was confused. Why was she lying under a tree? Where was she? The panic subsided as everything came back to her, and then it returned with a vengeance. She hadn't left her father a letter. What would he think happened? Would he come looking for her? Would her sudden disappearance cause him to suffer emotionally to the point that he died?

What had she done?

Technically, she had done nothing yet. She could wake Daigo and ask him to take her back, to forget that she had ever asked him to bring her here. But if she did that, then her father would surely die, and with a fate more gruesome than of a broken heart. As her mind whirled with concern, she heard soft pattering around her. It was sporadic at first, and then, without warning, the rain came.

It was a downpour, and before Lailani had the chance to get up, her clothes got soaked. She stayed where she was, not seeing the point of finding better shelter now. Curling into a ball, she pressed up against Daigo, but he was sound asleep. Her gown was soddened. She flung it away and buried her head into the crook of Daigo's foreleg.

She dozed in and out of sleep as the storm continued to rage, continuously jerking awake when thunder cracked the sky. By the time the sun rose on the horizon, the rain had stopped. Lailani was in a foul mood, cold, and wet. It was the worst kind of combination. Daigo stirred and awoke. He lifted his head and regarded her curiously.

*It did rain. This old nose still has it.*

L AILANI'S STOMACH GROWLED. She was hungry, but she hadn't brought any rations with her. That was one of many things she didn't take into consideration the night before. She hoped the camp would have breakfast available. If not, her mood would be even worse than it was now. Her clothes still weren't dry despite sitting near the fire that Daigo had made for her, but she was starting to get warm.

*I hope breakfast is still hot when we get to the camp,* she said. *I'm starving.*

*There's something I didn't tell you.*

*What's that?*

*Since you are going to take your father's place as his son, they will know you aren't already a rider, and thus not bonded to a dragon.*

*How would they know that?*

*The school keeps meticulous records,* Daigo replied. *They will not know that you aren't his child, but they will know that you don't have a dragon of your own.*

*I'll just tell them I have you.*

*You can't. They require riders to be bonded to their dragons. I am bonded to your father, and we can only bond with one human.*

*How will they know we aren't bonded, though?*

*As I said, they keep meticulous records. The only way to be bonded with a dragon is to go through the school. Well, there are other ways, but they are not sanctioned by the empire.*

*What do we do then?*

*I've been thinking about that. I will wait until nightfall, and then I will sneak into the stable. Once they start the bonding ceremony, you'll need to make sure that you choose me.*

*What if someone else chooses you first?*

*That is a risk that we run, but for a bond to be forged, both the dragon and the human must agree to the connection. If someone else chooses me, I shall refuse them.*

Lailani rubbed her hands together over the flames of the fire and nodded.

*You should get ready.*

*I am ready,* she replied, rising to her feet.

*You need to put on your armor.*

She grabbed her bag and removed the armor, laying the foldable cuirass on the ground. It was made of small silver square and rectangular plates that were connected by black chainmail and sewn to a beige leather backing. She slipped it on and was surprised that it was so light. It was also sturdy, offering plenty of protection from her neck down to her waist.

Lailani put the greaves on next, which were made of the same material as the cuirass, but they covered the length of her shins. The cuisses were attached via a belt and provided protection for her thighs. She strapped her sword on last.

*How do I look?*

*Like a warrior,* Daigo answered, and she could sense the pride in his words.

She felt empowered wearing the armor as if it could shield her from people's eyes as well as their weapons.

*A male warrior?*

*The dirt helps to hide your features. Did you bring the helmet as well?*

Lailani fished it from the bag and placed it over her head.

*That is better. It should be almost impossible for anyone to see that you are a woman now.*

*Good.* She stood in silence for a moment, not sure what to do.

*Take the scroll and go to the camp. Do not draw attention to yourself. I will enter the stable tonight and we shall see each other again soon.*

Lailani hugged Daigo's neck tightly.

*I pray I have not made a huge mistake,* she said.

*Only time will tell. Now go.*

Lailani retrieved the parchment with her father's summons and inhaled a deep breath. She turned in the direction of the encampment and trudged through the woods, wet leaves and mud collecting on her boots. Given that they were already loose and clunky, the sucking mud hindered her steps doubly so. She left the woods behind and continued across the tall grassy field to the front of the camp where a line of men had gathered.

Most of them were wearing armor, but there were a few who had either chosen not to or likely didn't own any. A rectangular table sat beneath a white canopy tent and two men in plain black kimonos with white sashes, Impressers, were checking people's papers. Lailani clutched her parchment tightly and studied the men around her. She was the shortest of everyone in line.

The men at the table worked efficiently, and before long, Lailani was next to hand her paper over. She tried to steady her breathing and remain calm, but her anxiety was causing her heart to race madly. The Impresser on the right waved her forward, and she walked up to the table.

"Conscription paper," he said, holding his hand out.

Lailani handed the parchment over. Her hand was tremoring, and she hoped he didn't notice. He read over the paper, looked at her, then looked back at the paper.

"Hayate Seijin?"

"That's my father. I've come in his place."

"Very honorable. Name?"

Lailani froze, eyes wide. She didn't have a name. Well, obviously she did, but she couldn't use her real name. The man looked at her expectantly.

"Lai," she said lowly.

"What was that?"

"It's Lai. Lai Seijin."

The Impresser crossed out her father's name and wrote hers above it using a bamboo brush and ink, then set it aside.

"You've been assigned to Lord Ishida's command. His pavilion is the large purple one. Everyone under his command is to use the rows of tents of the corresponding color. The school is providing meals throughout the day outside each lord's pavilion. You will eat, sleep, and train only with those of your clan. Any questions?"

Lailani shook her head.

"Very well. May your blade swing true."

The Impresser motioned for her to enter the camp. Lailani bowed to him and walked past the table, relieved that she hadn't encountered trouble. The camp looked completely different in the daylight. It was divided into four sections by large clearings, and each section had a towering pavilion. The section she'd been assigned to was purple as the Impresser had said, and the others were red, green, and black.

Lailani walked past the pavilion and paused. That was the same tent she'd stolen her clothes from. Her eyes widened at the realization that she'd stolen from a lord, and not just any lord, but the one she was to serve under. She swallowed hard and wandered among the rows of tents, looking for one that was open, but they all appeared to be taken. Were there more tents elsewhere?

"You look lost."

The voice was familiar, and she halted her steps. She slowly turned her head and saw Kalea.

"I'm sure we all look lost, though. Captain Shimura said we have to triple up on the tents. You're welcome to join ours." He hooked a thumb at the tent behind him and she spotted Huou stepping out of it. "I'm Kalea and this is Huou."

"I'm Lai," she said, trying to make her voice deeper. "Thank you for being so generous. I will gladly accept your invitation."

She walked over to where he stood and bowed. Her ancestors must have been watching over her. To be given a place among her friends was a fortuitous opportunity, but it was also risky. If they caught on to who she was … well, no bond of friendship overrode loyalty to the empire.

The two men were the same height, but that's where the similarity ended. Kalea's hair was as black as raven wings, and his eyes were an icy blue. He was thin but muscular, his facial features sharp and defined. Huou, on the other hand, had a bigger frame. He wasn't overweight by any means, but standing next to Kalea made him look twice as wide. His brown hair, short and thick, was styled in a bowl cut, and his green eyes offered a hint of mischief.

"You can put your things in the tent," Huou said. "We were just going to get something to eat."

"I am wearing everything I brought," Lailani replied sheepishly.

"No judgment here," Kelea chimed in. "We didn't bring much. Just our armor and some clothes. My father told me everything else will be supplied to us. Did you take your father's place as well, or are you a rider from the school?"

"I took my father's place. He is too old to fight."

"So is mine," Huou said.

Lailani smiled. She knew Huou's father, and while he was still in his prime, he'd been injured in a fishing accident and couldn't use his sword arm. Huou was probably trying to save his father from being dishonored, and she didn't blame him. She looked at Kalea.

"My father has an illness of the lungs. He can fight, but he can't breathe well, so I came instead."

Lailani knew that was true. "It sounds like we are all new to this, then. May we all return home safely when this is over."

"Agreed. Do you want to eat with us?" Kalea asked.

"Yes," she answered, and her stomach grumbled loudly, as if trying to join the conversation. Kalea and Huou chuckled.

"Come on. The Impresser said we could find food near the pavilion."

Lailani followed behind them, pleased that they didn't recognize her. She would need to come up with a false story about her past in case they asked her questions. Despite pretending to be someone else, she felt more at ease knowing she was with her friends from the island.

"How long will we be training?" she asked.

"A few months, from what I've gathered," Kalea said. "The Roarans have only just crossed the border into Terran, and the emperor's forces are already engaged with them."

"Then what are we here for?"

"We probably won't be needed, but we're being trained in the unlikely event that the Roarans defeat the others."

"If that happens, it won't matter how much training we've received," Huou said.

"Why not?" Lailani asked.

"Because the empire will have already fallen."

THE LINE FOR breakfast wasn't very long, and Lailani's mouth watered at the sight of the steaming food. She received the same thing as everyone else: a wooden bowl of soup and a chunk of grilled fish. The aroma of the soup was pungent, and she wrinkled her nose.

"What is this? It smells gross."

"You've never had miso before?" Kalea asked.

"No."

"It's tasty. I'm surprised that we're getting something other than rice or seaweed. They usually reserve stuff like this for the higher ranks."

Lailani had her doubts about the soup, but the fish looked delicious. She followed Kalea and Huou to an area where a large rug had been laid out. Many other soldiers sat on it, eating and talking amongst themselves. The three of them found a spot between two rowdy groups and sat down. Lailani removed her helmet, casting a wary look around.

No one cared.

She issued a silent prayer of thanks to her ancestors and quickly devoured the fish. It was fresh and delicious. She picked up the bowl and eyed the soup with uncertainty, hesitantly lifting it to her lips. Hunger drove her onward, and she took a small sip. Despite its smell, it had a toasty, salty-sweet richness.

Lailani downed the entire bowl before Kalea or Huou finished half their meal. They stared at her incredulously and she shrugged, offering an embarrassed grin.

"I didn't have dinner."

"No judgment here," Kalea said. It was a phrase he often used. "You can have the rest of mine if you want. I'm not very hungry. My stomach's been bothering me since I left home."

"You're not scared, are you?" Huou chided playfully.

"I won't lie. Yes, I am scared. This is the first time I've been away from the island, and the uncertainty of what awaits us is nerve-wracking."

Lailani was glad to know she wasn't the only one experiencing that feeling. She took Kalea's leftovers and finished them, sighing contentedly now that her stomach was no longer rumbling.

"So, where are you from?" Huou asked.

She knew the question would come up eventually, but she hadn't expected it so soon. Her heart raced as she panicked and tried to come up with something.

"We're from the Perched Cay," Kalea said.

Lailani leaned back, pretending to stretch, and her hand touched something wet. She glanced back and saw she'd stuck her hand in another person's bowl. Her eyes widened, and she jerked her hand away, knocking the bowl over and spilling some of the soup.

"Sorry," she muttered, then looked back at Huou. "I'm from—"

Before she could finish speaking, the person behind her roared angrily and grabbed the back of her armor, lifting her. She struggled to pull away, but whoever held her had a firm grip.

"You put your hand in my food, you fool," a deep voice said.

He whirled Lailani around and she looked up at the scarred face of a man so tall and thick, she felt like an ant in his presence.

"I-I'm sorry," she repeated. "It was an accident."

"A clumsy fool. Just what we need around here. Too bad the emperor requires the poor to be conscripted. You smell as dirty as you look."

The group of men he was with all smiled and laughed. Lailani's cheeks flushed warm with humiliation, and she shrank back.

"He cowers like a beaten dog. How will someone like you fight the Roarans?"

"Let him go," Kalea demanded.

"Are you his protector? Mind your own business."

"He apologized. What more do you want?"

The big man released Lailani and grabbed his bowl of soup, dumping what remained over her head. The warm liquid spread through her hair and dripped down the back of her neck. She clenched her jaw, doing her best to keep her mouth shut, but she desperately wanted to offer an angry retort.

"Watch yourself, boy. Next time I won't go easy on you."

Lailani straightened her cuirass and turned around, her cheeks still burning.

"Don't let people push you around," Kalea told her.

"He's as tall as a mountain and as muscular as an ox. All he'd have to do is hit me in the face and it would kill me."

"That's a little dramatic," Huou said. "He is a big one, but that doesn't mean anything. He's just a bully. You should say something."

If Lailani didn't know Huou from home, she would have no idea he was an instigator. He gave the impression that he was quiet and meek, but he was actually brash and a bit of a troublemaker.

"It's fine."

Huou frowned and stood up. He grabbed his bowl and stepped past Lailani, tossing the soup onto the man who'd apprehended her.

"What the …?" He sputtered and spun toward them, lunging for Huou since he was the closest. Huou sidestepped and tripped him. The big man stumbled and fell, crashing to the ground with a curse.

Chaos erupted as the other men jumped up and began fighting with Kalea and Huou. Lailani joined the fray without thinking, swinging her small fists and connecting a few blows, though she wasn't sure who she struck.

The giant man got back onto his feet and came for Lailani, grabbing her by the neck with his left hand. He lifted his right hand, balled it into a fist, and drew it back. Lailani blocked her face with her hands, but she could see through the space between her fingers.

"What is the meaning of this?"

The man stiffened, and Lailani noticed the chaos had ceased. No one spoke, and everyone that had been eating on the rug was now looking behind her. Her oppressor quickly released her and dropped to his knees, bowing his head. Lailani gently rubbed her neck and turned around to see who had spoken.

She sucked in a breath.

The most handsome man she'd ever seen was striding toward her. His armor was similar to hers but much newer. It lacked the lines of wear and tear, and the metal pieces gleamed under the sunlight. He sported a top knot of thick black hair, but unlike some of the other riders she'd seen, he did not shave the pate of his head. He stopped directly in front of her, his brown eyes full of fire.

"Bow to me," he commanded.

Lailani didn't even hesitate. She dropped down and lowered her gaze to his boots, her heart thundering in her ears. She swallowed hard, fearing that she was in trouble.

"Who is responsible for this infighting?"

"It was him, my lord," Kalea answered.

Lailani didn't dare look back. She kept her eyes locked on Ishida's boots. After a moment of silence, he stepped around her. A droplet of soup slowly trickled down the side of her neck, tickling her, and she struggled to stay still.

"What is your name?"

"Doi," the big man said.

"Tell me, Doi. Why do you sow dissension among my ranks?"

"My apologies, my lord. That fool put his hand in my food and I let my anger get the better of me."

"I see. Are you an Impresser, Doi?"

"No, my lord."

"Let this be a warning to you all, my *only* warning. The next man who thinks to use violence against his fellow will find his head departing from his body, courtesy of my blade. Is that understood?"

"Yes, sir!"

"Everyone, resume your meal. Except for you."

Lailani could feel the lord standing over her.

"Rise and come with me."

He walked away and Lailani rushed to her feet, hurriedly following after him. Did he know that she'd stolen from him? Or did he see through her façade and knew that she was really a woman? She grew anxious as they walked toward his pavilion. Two guards posted on either side of the entrance bowed their heads as he strode past them and into the tent. Lailani hesitated at the entrance for only a moment, then continued inside.

"What is your name, soldier?" He stood behind a large square table covered with a map and sculpted wood figurines.

"Lai Seijin."

"You are small, Lai. This will give many cause to belittle you. Some, like Doi, will even attempt to physically assault you. You must not allow it. Do you know how to defend yourself?"

"No, my lord."

Lailani tried to recall his surname and struggled for a moment before remembering the Impresser had called him Lord Ishida. Now that she could look upon him, she realized they shared a similar stature. Perhaps he'd been bullied when he was younger, and he felt compelled to give her advice on how to handle it.

"You will soon enough. We have a few months to train, and when the time comes for us to march, you will be well equipped for war. The next time someone tries to bully you, stop them."

"Yes, my lord."

"You are dismissed."

Lailani offered a bow and left, heading back to rejoin Kalea and Huou. She appreciated Ishida's advice, but she couldn't help wonder if that was the real reason he singled her out. She would need to keep her head down in case he was suspicious of her.

W HAT WAS THAT about?" Kalea asked when Lailani sat down.

"He told me to stand up for myself."

"So, the same thing we told you to do. Perhaps not everything whispered about him is true."

"What things are whispered about him?"

Kalea lowered his voice and leaned forward. "I've heard that he was raised by wild dragons."

"I've also heard that," Huou said. "And that he saved the life of the emperor. Twice. He killed an entire clan of assassins by himself—with his bare hands."

Lailani lifted her left brow questioningly. "And you believe that?"

Huou shrugged. "It's possible, but probably not true. There have been warriors in the past who've been known to master *bujutsu* to the point that they were all but invincible. Perhaps our lord has done the same."

Lailani's gaze went to the purple pavilion. "Perhaps," she whispered. "Those are heroic deeds, though. You made it sound like people say ill things about him."

"There's plenty of that, too," Kalea said. "Supposedly, he had his younger brothers put to death."

"What for?" Lailani asked.

Kalea shrugged. "For sport, maybe? No one knows."

"I hope that's not true. If he would so easily kill his own family, then what would he do to one of us if we failed in our training?"

"That's a fair question," Huou said. "And a good reason not to fail."

Lailani was once again questioning her decision to come in her father's place. She wanted to talk with Daigo, to hear his reassuring words, but he was too far away for her to connect her mind with his.

"When do we get to bond with dragons?" she asked.

"After we've proven ourselves in training," Kalea replied.

"How long will that take?"

"A couple of weeks, if I had to guess. My father said that with the looming threat of invasion, it might be quicker than that."

Lailani did her best not to look downcast. Weeks? She'd assumed it would only take a few days, and she certainly hadn't expected to be without Daigo that long. Kalea and Huou were her friends as well, but they didn't know she was among them, masquerading as a man.

"What kind of dragon do you want to bond with?"

Kalea's question shattered her reverie. She pictured Daigo's blue scales in her mind, his gray pupils—how they always pierced her soul!—and his ferocious-looking face.

"A blue dragon," she answered.

"That's the color I want to bond with also," Kalea said, smiling. "My friend's father back on the island is bound to a blue. I've only seen him a few times, but he's a beautiful dragon. I know it sounds odd to call a male dragon beautiful, but there is no other word I can think of."

"I understand. I feel the same way towards them. What about you, Huou?"

"Green," he said without hesitation.

"A nice choice, though I knew you were going to say that," Kalea said. "May we all get the dragons we desire."

"Here, here," Huou said.

"Where two or three agree, let it be," Lailani added.

Kalea gave her an odd look, and she realized her error.

"My friend says that, too. You remind me of her in a way."

"I remind you of a woman?"

"Well, no. Sorry, I didn't mean to insult you."

Lailani laughed. "You didn't. I was just messing with you."

"Silence!"

The command cut through the air above the noise, and all eyes turned to a man standing at the edge of the rug. His armor was the same style as Lord Ishida's, but it was entirely black. The blade sheathed at his side was the same color, and the man had the bearing of one who gives commands and didn't take any.

"I am Shimura, captain of Lord Ishida's forces. I hope you have finished eating because breakfast is over. Pile your bowls together and line up. You belong to me now."

Everyone scrambled into motion. Lailani hurriedly grabbed her bowl, along with Kalea's and Huou's, and added them to the growing pile in the center of the rug. She joined the line and waited nervously for the rest of the men to follow suit. Shimura led them on a march to the field outside of the camp and divided them into two rows.

Lailani stared at the man across from her. He was a foot taller than her, but he was as thin as she was, if not more muscular. He was bald and tattooed down the center of his head was a long black line. She tried not to stare at him and glanced down the line, noting that Kalea and Huou were on the same side as the tattooed man.

"Not every battle consists of weapons," Shimura said. "Some require wits, and others require the brute force of your hands. Measure the person across from you. That will be your opponent. I want to see your hand-to-hand skills. I will give the top five fighters a small command of men. A clan within a clan, so to speak. Each of them will choose the warriors they want, and there is no trading afterward. A warning to you all: do not dishonor yourself. I want to see fair fights."

The tattooed man stared intensely at Lailani, and her heart started racing. She didn't know how to fight. Her father never taught her the ways of war, perhaps because he assumed she would never need to know them. Lailani clenched her jaw. She would have to learn one way or another. She just hoped it wouldn't hurt too badly.

"Begin."

The two groups converged, each pair of men giving ample space to the others around them. Lailani strode forward, pausing a few steps away from her opponent. His expression was serious, but there was something in his eyes that told her he was going to enjoy pummeling her. She knew she was going to lose, but that wouldn't keep her from doing her best. Balling her right hand into a fist, she stepped in close and swung upward at his face.

The man was quick. His hands twirled around one another and he slapped her blow aside, then drove the flat end of his right palm into her throat. She staggered back and tripped over her own feet, landing hard on her back as she tried to gasp in a breath. Her throat hurt like a dozen bees had stung her.

"Get up!" Shimura shouted at her.

Lailani pushed through the pain and got back on her feet, rubbing her neck. Her opponent had a smug look plastered on his face, and it angered her. She swung with both hands this time, flailing wildly and without precision. Again, he slapped her strikes aside, but instead of landing his own blow, he used her momentum against her and sent her careering past him.

She crashed to the ground face-first, taking in a mouthful of grass. Lailani sputtered and spit it out as she stood up. A glance at the other groups revealed the matches were more even, and no one was on the ground. What if she didn't have what it took to be a warrior? Would they send her home and request her father to come? She didn't know, but she refused to let that be an option.

Her opponent was fast and trained in *bujutsu,* both of which she lacked, but that didn't mean he was invincible. The way he moved his hands was mesmerizing. His legs, however, were slower. Not much, but enough that it gave her an idea. She came at him again, but this time, she feigned a blow toward his head. As expected, his hands became a blur of motion as he moved to block her.

Lailani ducked down and threw herself backward, launching her right leg at the man's knee. She had him. At least, she thought she did. He spun out of reach and grabbed onto her ankle, jerking her toward him with one hand and cracking his other into the side of her leg. She screamed in agony, feeling something *snap* out of place. Her opponent released her and looked away in silence.

Through the dizzying pain, she saw Shimura kneel beside her. He inspected the damage to her leg and cast a furious look at the tattooed man.

"I didn't use my full strength," he said.

"Then his bones must be weak. Go get Lord Ishida's healer."

Shimura looked her in the eyes and placed a steadying hand on her shoulder.

"Breathe and focus on my face," he said. "He broke your leg, but it will be healed. Lord Ishida has the best healer in the empire."

None of his words made any sense to Lailani. The pain was so excruciating that she thought her spirit had left her body. It seemed to her as if she were floating just above her body, but that, too, made little sense to her.

Everything else became disjointed. She saw a woman clad in white, felt a multitude of hands bracing her, holding her in place. The woman touched Lailani's leg, jerking it roughly, and then the pain faded amidst the darkness that overtook her.

8

W HEN LAILANI CAME to, she was lying on a bedroll inside a tent. Two people were murmuring, and she propped herself up on her elbows to see Kalea and Huou sitting beside one another. A paper lantern burned in the corner, flooding the tent with warm, flickering light. They both turned to her and smiled.

"How are you feeling?" Kalea asked.

"I don't have any pain in my leg," Lailani replied, surprised. She looked at it and flexed the muscles. It was completely healed. "How did I get here?"

"You passed out after the healer set your leg. She used her magic to heal you, and Shimura had you brought here to rest."

"I guess that means I lost my match."

"Yes, but a broken leg is a good reason for losing," Huou said.

"You did well, regardless. Your opponent was a Senshi. That you lasted as long as you did was nothing short of a miracle."

"What's a Senshi?" Lailani asked.

"A warrior-monk. They spend years in silence training in the ways of battle. They are fierce combatants."

Lailani digested Kalea's words and quickly realized she was lucky to be alive. Her fight had been a training exercise, but if it had been real … she likely wouldn't be among the living anymore.

"I need to try harder," she said.

"Don't be so hard on yourself," Kalea replied. "It's only the first day, and we've got months of training ahead of us."

She supposed he was right, but still. To pull off being a man, she had to be stronger. If someone could break her leg with merely a punch, then she would not make it home in one piece.

"When is lunch?" she asked, changing the subject.

Kalea and Huou exchanged looks.

"You missed it," Kalea said.

"And dinner," Huou added.

Lailani turned her eyes to the tent opening. There was no light shining through the flaps.

"It's dark already?"

"Yes," Kalea said. "The healer said you probably wouldn't gain consciousness until morning. Looks like you are stronger than she thought."

An unexplainable weight was resting on her, heavy and suffocating. She could feel her eyes welling with tears and needed to escape.

"Where are the dragon stables?" she asked.

"At the north end of the camp. Why?"

"I need to get some air. I'm going for a walk."

"Do you want some company?"

"No, I'm fine. I'll be back soon."

Lailani rose from the bedroll and stepped out of the tent. The night air was warm, and the sky overhead was clear. A multitude of stars shined across the black canopy, and Lailani trekked through the camp under their light. She easily found the stable. It was an enormous wooden structure on the edge of the camp. While its size was impressive, it didn't seem big enough to house enough dragons for all the soldiers in the camp. A trio of guards was on duty, and she walked past casually as if the building wasn't her focus.

*Daigo?*

A host of dragon minds barraged her, and she paused in her steps to push them all away. None of them were Daigo's, and she sighed. Perhaps he was still waiting to sneak into the stable. She continued walking until the guards were no longer visible, then glanced around to ensure no one else was around. Satisfied, she climbed over the makeshift fence that surrounded the building and hurried over to the nearest stall.

Lailani peered inside and saw the partial shadowy shape of a dragon. It was mostly hidden in the darkness, but she saw the brief glint of red scales. Crunching footsteps caught her ear, and she froze. The familiar sound of Lord Ishida's voice drifted on the air, and she quietly slipped inside the stall with the dragon. A set of glowing eyes stared at her from the shadows, and she held her breath.

*Forgive my intrusion,* she said. *I need a place to hide.*

The dragon didn't reply.

"It was just the one injury?" Lord Ishida asked.

"Yes, sir," Shimura answered.

"It is only the first day of training."

"Yes. I believe the one responsible was a little rougher than he should have been. Lady Narumi healed the injured one and he should make a full recovery."

"That is good, though I fear this is an omen of what is coming."

"You've never been one for superstitions."

"No, and I still am not swayed by them. You know what I'm referring to. The Roarans are pushing the imperial forces back further every day. The emperor projects strength and confidence, as he should, but it is a façade. You know as well as I do that the power of the empire is on the decline. Our allies in Osnen continue to try and convince the emperor to merge with them, but he is stubborn and set in his ways."

"Surely you don't fault him for it. Our cultures are vastly different, and our history with the kingdom of Osnen isn't all peaceful."

"I do not envy his position, nor the decisions he must make. It is easy for me to cast judgment because I am not the one who bears the weight of an empire."

Lailani stood completely still, breathing as softly as she could manage. The dragon continued to stare at her in silence, occasionally offering a lazy blink.

"What of the men under your command?" Shimura asked. "Do you think they measure up?"

"That is yet to be seen. I will know by the end of the week who is going to make it, and who is going to leave without honor."

"Will you truly send them away knowing we need them?"

"Would you have me send them to their death? That is what awaits those who don't have what is necessary."

"That might be what awaits even those who do."

"I do not wish to dwell on such things. My dreams are troubled enough as it is."

"Very well. If you do not need anything, I will retire for the night."

"Get your rest. You have a lot of work to do tomorrow."

"Goodnight, sir."

Lailani heard Shimura leave, but Ishida was still there. The door to the stall opened and Lailani shrank back against the wall. Ishida stepped in and walked up to the dragon and laid a hand on its snout. A long moment of silence passed before he turned and left. Lailani exhaled in relief and closed her eyes.

*You shouldn't be here.*

Lailani snapped her eyes back open and met the dragon's glowing gaze. She swallowed hard and tried to calm her thundering heart.

*I know,* she replied. *I'm sorry. I only came to keep my father safe.*

*No, you shouldn't be* here. *Ishida will not be happy to find you near me.*

*Are you bonded to him?*

*I am.*

*I'm sorry,* she said again. *I'll leave now. Thank you for not revealing my presence.*

Lailani opened the door and stepped out, casting a glance behind her.

*If I may be so bold as to ask you a question. Are the things said about Ishida true? Did he really kill his brothers?*

*It is not for me to say, but there is much about him that is not as it appears.*

That only added more questions for her, and her curiosity toward him increased as well. She waved to the dragon and made her way through the camp back to her tent. Huou was asleep on his mat, but Kalea was gone. Lailani removed her armor and set it on the floor, then crawled onto her bedroll. A moment later, Kalea entered the tent.

"I had to relieve myself," he said.

Lailani didn't need to know that. She nodded and laid down. Kalea blew out the lantern, casting the tent into darkness. She was determined to do better tomorrow. Her thoughts turned to her father. Had he figured out what she'd done? And if so, was he angry with her? She imagined he was, especially since she took Daigo with her. She sighed and closed her eyes, eventually falling into a fitful sleep.

When a horn startled her awake, she realized it was morning already. Kalea and Huou were gone, probably eating breakfast. She rose out of bed and put on her armor, then paused when a cramp shot through her side. Lailani groaned. She thought things couldn't get any worse, and she was wrong.

It was going to be much more difficult to hide being a woman.

L AILANI COUNTED THE days in her mind again. She wanted to blame the cramps on the magic used to heal her, but she knew it was the bleeding pain. It was early this time, and it was another thing she hadn't planned for. Her hasty decision was proving to have more hiccups than she realized was possible.

Foregoing breakfast despite the growling in her stomach, she left the tent and began roaming the camp. She needed to find some cloth, thick enough to hide the blood when it came, as well as a private place to deal with the issue.

*You. Girl.*

Lailani stopped in her tracks and glanced around. She'd been walking absently, her thoughts busy and chaotic like a storm. The stable was on her left. It was more imposing in the daylight, and she spotted the head of a dragon gazing out from one of the stalls. It was the red one, Lord Ishida's dragon.

*Come here.*

*Me?* Lailani looked around again, but there was no one else nearby.

*Yes.*

*Didn't you warn me to stay away from you last night?*

*I did.*

She was confused. The dragon was now giving her a conflicting command. With cautious steps, she walked nearer to the stall. A trio of guards, possibly the same ones from the night before, was engaged in a game of dice and didn't notice her presence.

*I have something for you.*

*What is it?*

*Come inside and I'll show you.*

Lailani hesitated at the stall door. Was this a trick? Some sort of trap so that the dragon could eat her as punishment for the previous night? And then something occurred to her. When the dragon called to her …

*How did you know?*

*That you are a woman? I can smell the difference. Hurry, before the guards see you.*

Daigo never mentioned that fact. What if another dragon reported her presence to Lord Ishida? The red dragon drew back from the door and Lailani lifted the hatch and stepped inside. A sack lay on the ground and the dragon nodded to it. Lailani knelt and opened the sack, peering inside.

"Sea sponges?" She said the words aloud without realizing it.

*For your bleeding time. The scent was strong last night. It is stronger now.*

*Why would you show me such kindness? And why would you keep my secret?*

*We all have secrets.*

*Yes, but mine can bring about death, especially to those who knowingly aid me.*

*I am aware of that, which is why I have nothing to gain by revealing who you really are.*

*What do you gain by helping me?*

The dragon blinked, languidly stretching her bulk out along the stall. *What do you have to lose by letting me?*

*Nothing, I suppose.* She paused. *Thank you.*

*Tell me, how do you plan to bond with a dragon during the ceremony? Certainly, you know that none of us will willingly bond with a woman since the law forbids it.*

*I know. I have a plan in place.*

She dared not reveal anything more, in case the dragon was just prodding her for information. Daigo told her the world was a cruel place, and she wasn't sure who she could trust.

*I hope it is flawless. You have a kind heart, and I would hate to see you executed.*

*How do you know I am kind? You don't know anything about me.*

*I can sense it.*

Lailani stared the dragon in the eyes. There was no malice in her gaze. Perhaps she *could* trust this dragon. Only time would tell.

*Thank you again,* she said. *I am indebted to you.*

*I can hear the grumblings of your hunger. You should go eat before training starts. Each day will be progressively harder, and you won't survive on an empty stomach.*

Lailani grabbed the bag and left the stall, pushing the door closed behind her. She hastened across the camp and stashed the bag of sea sponges under her bedroll, then got a tray of food and joined her friends on the rug.

"Morning," Kalea greeted. "I trust your leg is still feeling good?"

"It is. I can't even tell anything was ever wrong with it."

"Lord Ishida's healer did well, then."

Lailani ate in silence. She thought about the conversation she overheard the night before between Lord Ishida and Shimura and was tempted to bring it up but decided against it. It would require explaining how and why she was privy to it, and it was more trouble than she thought it was worth.

"I assume I was the last one to be picked by the winners yesterday?" she asked.

"One of the first, actually," Huou replied. "Kalea here earned one of the five spots and chose you. We get to call him Talon Leader, now."

"Really?"

"Really," Kalea confirmed. "It took a lot of bravery to face a Senshi. Even if you were an experienced warrior, it would have been almost impossible to defeat him."

Lailani was glad to know at least one person thought she was brave. It boosted her confidence, but it also made her question why such a warrior was here for training. She voiced that question aloud.

"Learning to fight is important, but he is here for the same reason most of us are. Imperial edict aside, it's about bonding with a dragon. My father said there's nothing else like it in life."

Lailani's father had said the same thing many times as well. Bonding with a dragon was a lifelong commitment that came with many benefits and few disadvantages. For Lailani, there were no disadvantages to being lifelong friends with a dragon. She and Daigo couldn't bond for obvious reasons, but she would take what she could get.

"I miss him," Kalea said.

"Your father?"

He nodded. "I've never been away from home for more than a day."

"I've never been away from home at all," Lailani admitted. "I've lived my entire life in the same place around the same people."

"You sound like us," Huou said. "I miss my family, but I'm glad to get away and see the world. I don't like that we're going to war, but hopefully, we'll see exciting things along the way."

Lailani missed her father terribly, but she knew it was a small price to pay to keep him safe. And alive.

"You'll get plenty of adventure," Kalea said to Huou. "Once we're bonded, we're in the service of the empire until we die."

Lailani frowned. "My father retired from being a rider. He did his duty, but when the emperor recalled him, I knew he would die if he had to fight again."

"Few are allowed to retire. Was your father injured?"

"No," she replied. "His dragon was."

"Oh. I'm sorry to hear that."

"It's all right," Lailani said. "He lives a good life on the isl—" She caught herself. "—at home."

Shimura approached the rug and silence fell over the men.

"Line up!"

Lailani crammed the rest of her food into her mouth and added her tray to the pile in the center of the rug, then joined the formation of men. Just as the day before, Shimura led them into the field outside of the camp and they separated into their groups based on the previous day's winners.

Shimura assigned the pairs at random, and this time, he matched Lailani with a man whose skin was dark and wrinkled by constant sun. He must not have had a son to take his place, for he was far older in years than any of the other men.

"Take it easy on me," the man said with a toothless grin.

"Only if you show me the same courtesy," Lailani replied, also smiling.

"Look at me. I probably couldn't hurt you if I wanted to."

Lailani doubted that, but she didn't argue the point. Shimura gave the command, and the pairs of men began their hand-to-hand fighting. Lailani stepped closer to the man and brought her right fist in for a strike at his chest. Her blow landed, forcing the man to stagger backward.

"Good one," he said. "Your form is weak, though. You punched with your arm instead of with your core. When you use your core, you can strike with more power. Here, like this."

He jabbed his first forward quickly, punching the air beside her. His stance was firm and his body lined up in a way that Lailani hadn't seen before.

"You look like you know what you're doing," she said.

"I served the empire in my youth, but not as a rider. I am familiar with *bujutsu*. I can teach you if you want to learn."

"If you weren't a rider, why are you here? I thought only riders were called into service?"

"My presence here isn't voluntary."

"None of ours is."

"No, but my situation is different."

"How?"

The man's smile faded. "I was once a general, serving the emperor directly until I fell out of his favor. I've been a slave ever since and I am here to fight against the Roarans, but I will not be given the opportunity to bond with a dragon."

"Why don't you run away?"

The man laughed. "I've tried many times. The Impressers always find me. There is no escaping the claws of the emperor."

"The emperor doesn't sound like a good person."

"He's not. If the Roarans succeed with their invasion and the empire falls, it will be a good thing."

S TOP STANDING AROUND!"

Shimura glared at Lailani and the old man.

"Find me later if you want me to teach you. For now, you must fight how you know best."

"I don't understand how making people fight each other is a form of training," Lailani said.

"It's not. They are using this as a way to see who will make strong soldiers and who will be fodder for slaughter. Now fight me, before we get in trouble with the captain."

Shimura had them fight for almost an hour before he allowed a break. Lailani felt like a fish out of water, flailing around without purpose. If this truly was the way to see who would be left to die on the battlefield, she would be one of them. It was aggravating. Perhaps if they invested the time to show each of them how to fight, they would all make good soldiers, but what did she know?

"Things are going better for you today," Kalea said as he came to stand beside her. He offered her a wooden cup filled with water, which she gratefully accepted.

"No broken bones, if that's what you mean, but this feels just as torturous. Mahiro told me this is all to see who will be a soldier and who won't."

"The old man?"

Lailani nodded. Although they had spent the last hour sparring, she also had time to speak with him and learned his name. Kalea glanced at Shimura.

"I suspected as much," he said. "The way this is unfolding makes little sense to me."

Lailani again wanted to tell him what she'd overheard the night before, but it would bring more questions than she wanted to answer.

"Is something wrong?"

"No, I'm fine. I just wish I knew what I was doing. Mahiro offered to teach me *bujutsu*. Maybe I should take his offer."

"He offered to teach you? That is a great honor. Those who know the art do not always share their secrets. *Bujutsu* offers many things, and power is one of them. Most people don't enjoy sharing power."

His words reminded her of what Daigo told her. The world was a much darker and selfish place than she thought. Life on the island had kept her in the dark, and her eyes were slowly adjusting to the glare of reality.

"What if those who hold the power here have already decided which of us will die? What would be the point of having us bond with dragons?"

"I don't know," Kalea admitted. "There are many mysteries. Perhaps we'll soon find out. Lord Ishida said he's expecting a messenger to arrive today with an update from the front lines."

Shimura called for the groups to reconvene. Lailani hurriedly drank the rest of the water in her cup and returned it to the water trough, then followed Kalea to where the others were gathering. Once everyone had returned, Shimura motioned with his hand and several young boys brought a bo to each man.

Lailani gripped hers with her left hand and ran the fingers of her right one over the smooth wood. It had been polished, but it wasn't slippery. They had barely begun hand-to-hand, and now they were moving on to weapons?

"The bo is the oldest weapon of the Terranese people. Its length gives the advantage of striking from afar, and using it builds your hand-eye coordination. It serves its purpose, but a sword is better. I don't need anyone losing a limb, so we'll start with this. Pair up and get a feel for the balance of your weapon."

Kalea lifted his horizontally and put his right hand near the center, palm upward. The bo remained stable. Lailani mirrored his example. She managed to get the same result, and while the weapon was well balanced, it was heavy. Her muscles strained after a few moments and she was forced to rest one end of the bo on the ground. She massaged her arm, then lifted the weapon and took a few practice swings.

The heft was a problem for her, and she felt like an awkward child, but there was something about holding a weapon that gave her a feeling of power. With training, she would no longer be a lowly girl from the Perched Cay. She would be a warrior. Perhaps when the invaders were driven back and the war was over, her father would be proud of her.

*One step at a time,* she told herself.

"Want to partner with me?" Kalea asked.

"Do you know how to use one of these?"

"Somewhat. My father gave me a few lessons when I was younger, but I'm sure my skills are lacking."

Lailani held her bo with two hands near the center. Kalea shook his head.

"Hold it like this."

He turned slightly away from her and placed one end on the ground, then wrapped his right hand upside down around the other end.

"This is called fist eye down," he said. "This is the opening stance."

Lailani emulated his posture and nodded.

Kalea turned to face her, keeping the end of the staff on the ground in place. It lined up with his right foot. Again, Lailani copied the movement.

"This stance will allow you to kick the bo into your other hand, like this."

Kalea drew his right leg back and kicked the end touching the ground. It flew forward, and he grabbed it with his left hand. Lailani did the same.

"You are on the offensive. I will attempt to block your strike. Step forward and swing the bo behind you, sweeping it up and around, and strike downward at me."

Lailani ran his instructions through her mind's eye, envisioning the attack. She took a breath and swung the bo backward on her left side, angling it up like rowing a boat, and continued forward with the momentum, her left hand leading the end of the bo toward Kalea's head. He raised his bo to meet hers, resulting in a loud *clack*.

"Not bad," he complimented. "You need to use your core. When you only use the force of your arms, it's too weak. An enemy will be able to block and recover quickly. Using your core will add more power to the blow, and it can offset your opponent's balance."

There was the word again. Core. Lailani wasn't sure what it meant. Was this something all men knew about? And if it was, would it be foolish of her to ask for an explanation? The fear of being discovered was enough to keep her mouth shut.

"Now do it again, but faster."

Lailani stepped back from him and got into the opening stance. Once Kalea was situated, she kicked the bo into her hand and did the same movements as before. She put more force into her strike, and when Kalea blocked it, the force reverberated through her arms. It was a distinctly odd feeling.

"That was better, but you still didn't use your core. Don't be afraid to hurt me. I can handle it."

Lailani felt her cheeks flush with warmth. He thought she wasn't trying hard enough, but she'd used all of her strength in that attack. She had a longer path than she thought if she wanted to be a warrior.

"Let's switch," Kalea said. "I'll show you how I strike, and you block. This way, you know what it's like being on both sides."

They both returned to the opening stance. Defending looked easier than attacking, and Lailani was confident she could block Kalea. She kicked the bo into her hand again and brought it up horizontally, her grip firm. The end of Kalea's bo came at her with lightning quickness. She braced herself and watched dumbly as her elbows folded under the blow, her staff crashing into her chest. Kalea's bo struck next, smacking her diagonally across the face. A grunt escaped her lips as she fell onto her back.

Kalea knelt over her. "Are you all right?"

"I'm fine," she lied. Her face was burning and her eyes were watery, both from the pain and the desire to cry. Kalea offered her his hand, and she accepted, getting back on her feet. She blinked repeatedly to clear the tears and rubbed at her forehead.

"You're still not using your core. It's all right if you don't know how, but you'll need to learn."

"Let's try again," Lailani said. "I won't be much of a warrior if I can't block a wooden staff."

"You're not wrong," Kalea chuckled. "If you want to make it to the bonding ceremony, you need to be able to fight."

Fear wriggled in her gut, and she nodded. Failure wasn't an option. She had to succeed in this to keep her father safe. They went through the sequence again and again. Each time she tried to block, she got a hard rap on her face, hand, or shoulder. Bruises were the least of her worries. She continued, despite the pain and humiliation. Kalea offered for them to switch and let her take the offensive again, but she refused. In her mind, until she could defend herself, she had no right to practice her attack.

A shadow passed overhead, disrupting everyone. Lailani turned her eyes upward and saw a massive wingless black dragon. The beast descended near the stable and those around her began whispering. The messenger from the front lines had arrived.

"You're all dismissed for now," Shimura ordered, then strode back to the camp.

Lailani slumped to the ground, thankful for the break. Her knuckles throbbed with agony, but it didn't distract her attention from the messenger. The one who came to the island had brought bad news, and her stomach twisted with anxiety at the memory.

"Let's pray for good news," Huou said as he joined them. "I'm not ready to die yet."

11

N O ONE IS going to die on my watch," Kalea said. "Not if I can help it, anyway."

"I was joking," Huou replied. "There's too much of the world to see to die this young. Besides, I'm sure the imperial army is giving those Roaran scum a beating. It wouldn't surprise me if that messenger has come to announce our victory."

Lailani opened her mouth to say something, then hurriedly clamped it shut. From what she'd heard, it sounded like the imperial army might not be able to stop the Roarans, and that meant they would all see battle. She prayed to her ancestors that was not how things were going.

"I'm hungry," Kalea changed the subject. "Do you think lunch is ready yet?"

"Only one way to find out. You coming?" Huou asked Lailani.

"I need water more than food," she said, standing. She brushed off her trousers and winced. Her hands were raw and blistered, and the pressure in her head was threatening to give her a headache.

They walked together back to the camp and joined the line near Lord Ishida's pavilion. The fare today was seaweed and rice. Lailani followed Kalea and Huou to the meal rug and sat down. She ate sparingly, feeling as though she was going to be ill. It didn't help that her bleeding time was upon her, adding to her discomfort.

Her thoughts turned to how Lord Ishida's dragon had brought her the sea sponges. The dragon knew she was a woman, yet still helped her and didn't tell Lord Ishida about her. It was a curious thing, and she made a mental note to ask Daigo about it later.

A raucous erupted on the other side of the camp. Lailani turned her attention in that direction, but she couldn't see anything. The other men in the clan began standing and trying to see what was happening.

Lailani looked from Kalea to Huou. "What do you think that's about?"

"I don't know," Kalea replied.

"Let's find out," Huou said. He hurried to his feet and headed off, leaving his unfinished meal behind. Emboldened by his departure, a few other men followed after him.

"I bet it has something to do with the messenger."

Kalea nodded. "Probably."

He looked calm, but Lailani could see her own fear echoed in his blue eyes. At least she wasn't alone in being afraid. They sat in silence and waited. Those who left returned, including Huou, and people began talking excitedly.

"Lord Katsuo and his men have been called to the front lines," Huou said.

Kalea's face scrunched oddly. "How? The bonding ceremony hasn't happened yet."

"The imperial army is suffering heavy casualties. The emperor is calling for reinforcements. I think he chose Lord Katsuo because his men are the most battle tested. Most of them are former soldiers."

"It makes sense to send them even though they don't have dragons," Kalea mused. "Though without the power of the dragons, it's like trying to stem the flow of blood from a wound with rice paper. When do they leave?"

"They're packing up now."

Lailani decided it was no longer time to keep what she knew to herself. She cleared her throat and the other two looked at her.

"I may have overheard something," she said. "Lord Ishida was talking to Shimura. The empire is weak, and the Roarans might be successful in their invasion."

Kalea stared at her. "That would explain the request for support, but why aren't we all going?"

"They need dragons," Huou said. "By only pulling one clan away, that leaves the rest of us to continue training. We can get through the bonding ceremony, and we're more likely to make an impact when we're called to join the battle."

Lailani realized it was no longer a question of whether they would go to war, but when. Her stomach twisted again, and she gritted her teeth. She needed to learn everything she could. Rising to her feet, she scanned the crowd of men and found Mahiro. The old man was sitting by himself, eating his food as if nothing was happening. She walked to where he sat and knelt on the rug in front of him.

"Will you teach me *bujutsu?*"

Mahiro set his empty bowl aside and looked her in the eyes. "Do you fear the coming darkness?" he asked.

Lailani swallowed hard and nodded slightly.

"You are right to. I will teach you, but it takes years to master it. By the sound of things, we might have weeks. I will do what I can to impart my knowledge to you, but know that it will not be easy. We will have to practice after our formal training, which means little rest for either of us."

"I will do whatever I must," she said.

"Very well. Meet me in the field once we're dismissed by Shimura. It's going to be a long night."

"Thank you, Mahiro. I am indebted to you."

"I know what it means to be a slave to another, and I would never ask for repayment. Consider this a gift."

"I am honored," Lailani said, bowing her head to him. She got up and returned to her tent, sneaking the sack of sea sponges out from under her bedroll. Taking one, she hid it under her armor and pushed the bag back, then left the tent and trekked through the camp, looking for a private place.

A plain brown tent caught her eye. Next to it, two wooden posts supporting a thick cord stood like solitary guards. Wet linens hung on the cord, left out to dry under the sun. Lailani glanced inside and saw the tent was empty. She stepped in, took care of her cleansing, and then exited, glancing around. This part of the camp was desolate. She made her way back to the meal rug and saw that everyone was gone.

Cursing under her breath, she sprinted to the field and found the rest of her clan waiting for her. Shimura eyed her but said nothing.

"Word travels like wildfire, so I'm sure you've all heard the news. If you haven't, then listen closely. Lord Katsuo and his clan have been pulled to the front lines. Count yourselves fortuitous that you have been spared to continue learning. You're going to need it."

Lailani felt as though the captain aimed his words at her specifically, despite not looking at her.

"That's the good part. The bad? Your training has to be sped up. We face the possibility of being called into battle at any moment, so you must learn the ways of war at a faster pace than expected. That is the way of things sometimes."

Shimura motioned for the young boys who'd brought the bos earlier. This time, they brought swords. The metal blades glimmered under the sunlight, blinding those unfortunate enough to stare at them from the wrong direction. Lailani gingerly took the one offered to her. It wasn't as finely crafted as her father's sword and had several notches and scratches along the blade.

"Just as with the bo, you will need to get a feel for your blade. When you are ready, I will lead you all in a few sequences. Lord Ishida has been kind enough to give us his healer for the time being. I expect there will be many injuries. Lady Narumi is a talented healer and will be able to treat even the most grievous of wounds. With that said, try not to kill one another."

Lailani and the rest of the men spent a few moments swinging their swords about and finding the best way to hold them. Shimura unsheathed his blade from his waist and stretched, performing a few quick jabs. Lailani watched him intently, desperate to learn anything and everything she could.

The next few hours went by quickly, despite the heat of the sun and the rawness of her hands. At some point, her fingers became numb and she no longer felt any pain. Shimura led them through several ways of attacking and defending. She soaked it all in as if made of cotton wool, committing the most important things to memory.

It was early evening when he dismissed them. Every muscle in Lailani's body ached, and she wanted nothing more than to take a hot bath and get some rest, but she knew Mahiro was waiting for her. She went to the water trough and splashed her face, cleaning the sweat and grit away. Mahiro joined her and used one of the wooden cups to drink.

"Are you prepared?" he asked.

"I am."

"Good. Come with me."

Mahiro led her further into the field, away from the camp. The grass swayed gently as a breeze swept through the area. Lailani found it oddly peaceful. It was hard for her to fathom that somewhere far from here, a war waged for the fate of the empire.

"There are twelve forms of *bujutsu,* but we only have time for one. I have considered which form would best suit you, and I think I have decided."

"Which one have you chosen?"

"The Dragon form."

I T WAS LATE in the evening when Lailani stumbled into the camp. The moon glowed brightly in the clear sky overhead, illuminating her path. She was beyond exhausted. Between the beating she took from Kalea's bo and the multitude of hits Mahiro had landed, she was certain her skin would be covered in bruises.

The countless names of Dragon form movements swirled within her mind: Dragon Claw, Shield of Scales, Talon Forward, Talon Backward. *Bujutsu* was more complicated than she realized. The one move she had already memorized was the Shield of Scales. It was a form used to block. She absently rubbed a sore spot on her left arm; one of the many places Mahiro had struck her.

Angling her steps toward the stable, she navigated between the rows of tents and stopped when the building came into view. She needed to make sure Daigo had managed to sneak inside. The guards on duty weren't very alert. One was sitting on the ground, back against the stable. He appeared to be sleeping, but Lailani wasn't taking any chances. She crept slowly, every muscle in her body demanding she turn back and get some rest.

*Daigo?*

She waited. The longer the silence stretched, the more she became worried something had happened to him. If the guards had caught him, her entire plan was gone like dust in the wind.

*Little one,* his familiar voice greeted.

She breathed a sigh of relief. *Where have you been? I came last night and you didn't answer.*

*I had some trouble finding an opportunity last night, so I waited another day. When the last pair of guards switched out, I was able to get inside the stable. How is the training?*

*Grueling. Someone broke my leg.*

*What?* She couldn't feel his emotions, but the way the word entered her mind clearly conveyed his anger.

*I'm all right,* she said. *A healer fixed it. And I'm certain it was an accident. I'm small and weak, so it isn't hard for someone to hurt me. Today was better ... mostly. My muscles burn like fire.*

*You are not accustomed to pushing yourself so hard. After a few days, the soreness will fade. Things will get easier after that.*

*I hope so. I don't have a clue what I'm doing, and I fear I may not have what it takes to be a soldier.*

*Bah! You are cut from the same cloth as your father. With some practice, you will be a great warrior. You are small in stature, yes, but that means your enemies will underestimate you. Learn to use that to your advantage.*

*I will.* She remembered what Lord Ishida's dragon said. *There is someone here that knows I'm not a man.*

*They haven't betrayed you?*

*No. She offered to help me. It's my commander's dragon. She said she could smell the difference between men and women.*

*She is right. That is something I overlooked. We'll need to be careful that none of the other dragons find a reason to say something. That will work in our favor during the bonding ceremony. No dragon will want to bond with a woman, so they will shy away from you.*

His words stung her, but she knew he was only being truthful. No dragon would willingly put their life in jeopardy for a woman. Well, other than Daigo, anyway.

*And no human will want to bond with such an older dragon,* she said, smiling.

Daigo growled in response and changed the subject. *Who is this dragon you speak of?*

*I don't know her name. She's in the first stall at the end. A red dragon. There's something else. One of the commanders has been called to the front lines.*

*Before the bonding ceremony?*

*Yes. People say that the imperial army isn't faring well against the Roarans. We will almost certainly see battle.*

*I am no stranger to war. I'm sure you are afraid, but I will do my best to keep you safe. Your father would not be happy if I allowed you to get hurt.*

*If my deed hasn't killed him of heartache.*

*Do not say such things, little one. Your father would be proud of you. He* is *proud of you.*

Lailani wasn't so sure about that, but she didn't argue the point. *They've sped up our training as well. I suspect the bonding ceremony might happen sooner than we expected.*

*I'll be ready,* Daigo said. *Learn all that you can until then. I'll help you with anything you lack.*

*Kalea and Huou are here,* she added. *They've taken me in. It's nice to be around friends.*

*You play a dangerous game.*

*I am being careful. They do not suspect anything.*

*Yet. I can smell your blood. That will certainly give you away.*

*I have it handled.*

*I trust you do. You should rest. Morning will come quickly and your pains will not subside much.*

*Thank you for doing this,* Lailani said. *I know we are both risking our lives, but we have ensured my father is safe.*

*Don't thank me just yet. I may have sealed both our fates by agreeing to this.*

*That remains to be seen. I'm going to bed before I fall asleep standing here. Goodnight.*

*Goodnight, little one.*

Lailani somehow made it back to her tent and wearily slipped her boots off, but left her armor on and laid on her bedroll. She assumed Kalea and Huou were asleep. They hadn't moved and their breathing was steady and rhythmic. She closed her eyes and fell into darkness.

She awoke to something hard jabbing into her ribs. With a tired groan, she sat up and realized it was one of the metal plates of her armor. She slid out of bed and issued a hiss. Her muscles hurt twice as much as the day before. It took her a moment to put her boots on, and even longer to make it out of the tent.

The temptation to go back to bed pulled at her, but she pushed the tent flaps aside and stepped into the brisk morning air. A thick fog had fallen over the camp, and the chill gave her gooseflesh. She clasped her hands together and breathed into them as she walked, joining the line for food. It was the same as yesterday: seaweed and rice. She carried her bowl to the meal rug and gingerly sat with Kalea and Huou.

"You look like death," Huou said.

"Thanks," Lailani replied. "I'm sure you would too if you spent most of the night getting kicked and punched."

"Mahiro?" Kalea asked.

Lailani offered an *mhm* as she took a bite of her breakfast. At least her cramps had subsided. That was some respite, however small.

"We heard something interesting. The bonding ceremony might be moved back a few days."

"I thought that might happen," she said with her mouth full.

"That means they will cut our training short."

That gave her pause. "They intend to send us into battle to die?"

Kalea shrugged. "It's all rumor. Neither Shimura nor Lord Ishida have said anything official."

"Not yet," Huou said.

Lailani finished her meal and looked at Lord Ishida's pavilion. His dragon had told her that things were not as they appeared. Everyone thought him a tyrant, but from her limited experience with him, Lailani didn't think he was. Perhaps people mistook his rough rigidness for something else. He wouldn't send them to a needless death, would he?

The guards outside the pavilion lowered into bows, and Lord Ishida strode out, Shimura following behind him. Neither one looked happy. The captain hurried ahead of the lord.

"On your feet!" he shouted.

The meal rug became a chaotic mess as everyone rushed to stand, knocking over their bowls in the process. Shimura eyed the mess and turned to Lord Ishida.

"My lord."

"I am as surprised as you all by the orders brought by the messenger yesterday. We are in the midst of uncertain times, and the emperor has placed his trust in men like me to ensure we equip his armies to handle the threats Terran faces. I strive to bring honor to my family and my ancestors, but that is difficult to do when I am given less than ideal circumstances."

He shared a look with Shimura.

"The emperor has ordered the remaining clans here to begin with the bonding ceremony early. As such, training today will only last until noon, then you will prepare yourselves. By the time evening comes, you will all find yourselves bonded to a dragon."

13

L
AILANI WAS SHOCKED. She hadn't expected the ceremony to happen so suddenly. Lord Ishida returned to his pavilion, and Shimura gave them all a few minutes to digest the information.

"So, we'll be bound to a dragon by nightfall," Kalea said. "When I heard they might push the ceremony back, I didn't think it would be *this* quickly."

"Are you disappointed?" Huou asked.

"No, just surprised is all. And maybe nervous." He smiled, the left corner of his mouth twitching slightly.

"There's always a kernel of truth in a rumor," Huou said. "I just wonder who started it. Shimura doesn't seem like the type to let information like that out before it's been announced, but someone knew. Everyone heard the same thing as me."

"Maybe someone overheard a conversation as I did," Lailani offered. "They weren't exactly speaking in private when I overheard them."

Huou nodded. "That seems likely. This might be a sign we're going to war soon. Why rush the ceremony unless they need more men, and fast?"

"That's my thinking as well," Kalea grunted.

Lailani could tell by his sudden change of demeanor it troubled him. It troubled her, too, and she didn't have any words of encouragement to give him. She needed some herself. Shimura ordered them to march out to the field. Daigo needed to know what was going on, but she couldn't slip away to tell him now.

She walked with the others to the field and wondered what the captain had in store for them today. Nothing too strenuous, she hoped. Her muscles were still screaming at her. Shimura marched onto the field and stood quietly, his gaze roaming over everyone.

"You haven't experienced life fully unless you've bonded with a dragon," he finally said. "To share your thoughts and raw emotions with another being the way you do through the bond is … impossible to describe. It will feel odd at first, perhaps even invasive, but as time passes, you will grow accustomed to it."

Jealousy burned within Lailani. She wanted to know how that felt, but she never would. Daigo couldn't bond with her, and as he said, no dragon would risk their life to bond with a woman. She didn't know why, but tears filled her eyes. She wasn't a man, nor a warrior. And when the sun rose tomorrow, she wouldn't be a real dragon rider, either.

Everything about her was a sham. Shame washed over her, and she prayed to her ancestors they would forgive her.

"Today, we'll continue practicing with the sword. You will use what you learned yesterday to duel one another. Your Talon Leaders will assign you into pairs, but only one pair will spar at a time. Watch and learn from one another."

Lailani groaned. That was the last thing she wanted to hear. The boys from the day before trudged onto the field and handed out swords. Lailani took hers and gripped the hilt gingerly. The blisters on her hands flared with pain and she clenched her teeth, hissing in a breath.

"You all right?" Huou asked.

"I will be," Lailani replied.

Kalea assigned her to a man who looked too young to be enlisted. He was a little taller than her, and his slight frame and thin arms told her he wasn't used to manual labor. He offered a nod and watched the other men as they grouped together. Kalea and his opponent went first. The other gathered around them in a circle, offering friendly shouts of encouragement to them both.

They were evenly matched in skill, and the bout lasted only a few minutes before Kalea landed a hit on his opponent's chest. His armor prevented any injury from the strike, but had the fight been real, Kalea's strike would have been fatal. They bowed to one another and Kalea chose Huou to go next.

Whereas Kalea's movements were smooth, graceful even, Huou's were comprised of brute force. He battered his opponent mercilessly, and Shimura preemptively called an end to the match.

One by one, the pairs took their place, battling until there was a clear victor. Lailani knew she wouldn't win against her opponent. She could barely hold her sword without wincing. A full-on duel would only aggravate her discomfort, and she considered giving her opponent an easy victory.

A commotion amid one of the other clans erupted, and everyone turned to see what was happening. Lailani squeezed into the crowd of men who shared her curiosity as they huddled around the action. People jostled together and Lailani glimpsed a vibrant red stain on the grass.

"He's dead," someone whispered. "There's no recovering from a wound like that."

"Lord Ishida's healer can handle it," another said.

Given how the woman had healed Lailani's leg, she had to agree with the second man. The crowd parted to let Shimura and the healer through, and Lailani saw just how bad the scene was. One man was lying on the ground, covered in blood. His opponent stood a few feet away, a worried look on his face.

"I'm sorry, sir," he said to the captain. "He brought his sword up to block the way you showed us yesterday, but then something happened and my blade cut right through his wrist."

"Accidents happen," Shimura replied. "Everyone step aside and give Narumi some room."

Lailani watched the healer, Narumi, kneel beside the injured man. His right hand had been cut off at the wrist, and blood was spurting from the stump. She felt bile rise in her throat, but she swallowed quickly enough that she didn't vomit. The sight was horrifying.

Narumi wrapped a clean bandage over the wound and applied pressure, but she was frowning. She leaned over the man, peering at his chest. She turned her head and looked up at Shimura.

"He will not survive."

"What do you mean? Use your magic to stop the blood loss from his hand. He'll be fine. I've seen many men survive worse."

"His hand isn't the problem," Narumi said. "It's the chest wound."

Shimura stepped closer. Lailani was morbidly curious to see what the healer was talking about, but she kept her focus on Narumi. The sight of the man's bloody stump was already burned into her mind's eye. She didn't need a worse vision to replace it.

"You can't save him?"

"I'm trying, but his life force is fading faster than my magic can replace it."

"Try harder," Shimura demanded.

"I cannot. To go any further is to stray into the dark side of magic, which I am forbidden to do by the emperor's law. I am not a necromancer, my lord."

Shimura glared at her, but he said nothing. The man gasped in a breath and went still. The silence stretched, seeming to last an eternity before Narumi released the man's arm and rose to her feet. She bowed to Shimura and retreated from the field.

"Let this be a lesson to us all," he said. "Life can end at any moment. Let us offer a prayer to his ancestors."

Lailani bowed her head and prayed, asking that the man's spirit be found acceptable to join his ancestors in the afterlife.

"You are all dismissed. I will tend to Seto's body."

The men quietly left the field, only the sound of their steps and the rustling grass drifting in the air. Lailani didn't know Seto, but she felt pained by his death. He was so young, but the strand of his life had been cut short. She returned to her tent and climbed onto her bedroll, lying on her back. She stared at the wooden tent pole above her, tracing its length with her exhausted eyes.

She needed to tell Daigo about the bonding ceremony, but she didn't have the strength or the willpower to get up. Her eyes grew heavy and she closed them, thinking only to rest them for a moment.

"Lai. Lai, wake up."

Lailani startled awake and saw Kalea standing over her. She glanced around confusedly.

"What is it?"

"You dozed off," he said. "I didn't want to wake you, but they are serving lunch and it'll be the last meal until after the bonding ceremony."

She blinked several times and sat up, rubbing her hands over her face. "Thanks. I'd rather not miss another meal."

Rising from the bedroll, she followed Kalea out of the tent. She barely registered waiting in line or eating. She stared blankly at Lord Ishida's pavilion, the memory of Seto's handless arm spurting blood taking over her thoughts. A shudder wracked her body, and she pushed the image from her head.

"What if we can't do this?" she asked.

"Bond with a dragon?" Huou asked.

"No. This." Lailani waved her hand around. "All of this. What if we can't handle this? War, death … everything."

Huou looked at Kalea.

"It's a fair question. Everyone copes with it in their own way, but it can scar some worse than others. I suppose you have to ask yourself what you value the most, and remind yourself every day so you don't lose sight of *why* you're doing this. For me, it's so that my children, if I ever get blessed to have any, have a place to live in freedom."

Lailani nodded. Her moment of weakness faded, and she met Kalea's stare.

"I'm sorry for being weak," she said.

"Don't apologize. I admit freely to being afraid. There's nothing wrong with weakness."

Perhaps there wasn't, but Lailani despised the feeling. The fog in her mind cleared, and she was more alert. She would pretend to bond with Daigo, and she would continue to learn the ways of war. If the Roarans wanted a fight, she would be prepared to give it to them.

14

THE PREPARATIONS FOR the bonding ceremony were complete, and all three of the commanders and their clans had gathered in the field outside of the school. On the walk over, Lailani passed the spot where she thought Seto had died, but she wasn't sure because someone had cleaned the blood from the grass.

A pyre was erected in the center of the camp, and after the bonding ceremony ended, Seto's body would burn upon it so that his spirit could be free to join his ancestors, or if he was unlucky, to travel to the Island of Lost Souls. The night would end with a feast to celebrate both the bonding and to honor Seto's loss.

Overhead, a few dragons circled over the field, their riders keeping a vigilant eye on the proceedings. Huou said those riders were from the school. They were part of the imperial army but were not required to fight for the emperor. She wondered what made them so special that they were allowed to avoid war.

Although the multitude of men were all whispering to one another, it created a loud chorus of voices. The gates to the school swung open, and a man wearing a flowing yellow silk robe stepped out to greet them. The whispers ceased, and once it was completely silent, the man spoke.

"Welcome to my school," he said, raising his voice to be heard. "I am Master Satoshi. Your commanders are aware of my rules, but I will inform you all of them now. The school itself is off-limits to outsiders. Do not attempt to enter it. It is locked against you, and the consequences of trying to break in will be dire."

Lailani swallowed the lump in her throat. Was this place dangerous? And what did it have to do with the bonding ceremony? The dragons were in the stable at the camp. Master Satoshi continued, interrupting her thoughts.

"Your commander will lead you belowground under the school, and there you will find a dragon willing to bond with you. I offer you a warning: there are untamed dragons down there. If you choose one of them, they will fill your path with difficulty, but it is not an impossible road. You will not be able to discern them apart from the others except by their temperament, and by the time you experience their disposition, it will be too late to turn back."

Lailani's heart was pounding. She looked over her shoulder toward the camp. Daigo was back there. He needed to get below the school, but she couldn't communicate with him from this distance. She would have to return to the camp, but how? Shimura would be furious if she left without permission, and she doubted he would give her his consent unless the situation was important.

"Lord Kentato's clan will go first, followed by Lord Ishida. Lord Hisamatsu will go last. Do not worry about a lack of dragons. Lord Katsuo's premature departure means there are plenty available." Master Satoshi motioned with his hand. "Lord Kentato, if you will."

Lailani watched the commander and his clan file into the school's courtyard. Perhaps if she snuck away while no one was watching, she could get to the camp and let Daigo know he was in the wrong place. If she was quick enough, she'd return before it was Lord Ishida's turn. Her lips were dry, and she licked them nervously as she took a step backward.

"Watch where you're going," someone hissed.

"Sorry."

She turned around and saw the person she'd bumped into was from Lord Hisamatsu's clan. Bowing her head to him in apology, she hesitantly made her way through the crowd of men, the collective stench of their body odor enough to make her gag. When she broke free of the crowd, she increased her pace, speed walking until she was far enough away to break into a full run.

Reaching the camp, she skidded to a halt and looked for the guards that kept watch over the stable. She didn't see them, and she hurried over to the structure.

*Daigo? Daigo, where are you? You need to get to the other stable.*

There was no reply. At least, not from Daigo.

*Why aren't you at the school?* It was Lord Ishida's dragon. *And who is Daigo?*

Lailani wondered how much she could trust the dragon. She had aided her, but it could be a trick. She hesitated a moment, then decided to trust the beast.

*Daigo is my friend.*

*I assume he's part of how you plan to fit in with the rest of the riders?*

*Yes.*

It felt freeing to admit that, and some of the invisible weight she bore lifted. Lailani approached the dragon's door and pulled it open, glancing inside. She spotted the dragon's glowing eyes in the shadows near the back of the stall.

*You must be close indeed for him to risk his life for you. Are you bonded to him?*

*No, he's my father's dragon. He only agreed to come because it would keep my father from danger. He's not able to fight anymore. I came here for the same reason as Daigo.*

*Humans are intriguing creatures, capable of acts most foul, and yet loyal to a fault. My amazement never ceases.*

*Have you seen him? He's a blue dragon. Older, battle-scarred.*

*I have not, but he wouldn't be here, anyway. This stable only houses the bonded dragons of the commanders and their underlings.*

Lailani frowned. If Daigo wasn't here, then where was he? She'd spoken to him the night previous, and he'd told her he was in the stable.

"Blessed ancestors," she muttered, realizing her error. She sprinted back to the school, cursing her foolishness the entire way. She slowed to a walk as she drew close to the crowd and pushed herself through the mass of bodies, grimacing every time she touched a sweaty body.

"Where'd you go?" Kalea asked when she returned to her spot.

"To the back of the line. I needed some fresh air."

He smirked. "I doubt some of these people have bathed in a month. You learn to get used to it."

Lailani hoped she never got used to the stench of perspiring men. She reached out with her mind.

*Daigo?*

Nothing.

She was growing worried that something had happened to him. Lord Ishida's dragon could have been wrong. Maybe he had been in the other stable, but someone had found him. Worse, what if they knew why he was here? Her mind was rampant with anxious thoughts. This could be the end of her plan … unless she found a dragon willing to bond with her.

That seemed unlikely, but what if there was a dragon foolish enough to take the risk? Could she do

101

it? Of course she *could,* but would she? That was a question she didn't have an answer to. Although she wasn't bound to Daigo, she felt like that would be a betrayal of some kind. Perhaps she was overthinking things in her exhaustion. The sooner the ceremony was over, the sooner she could get some rest.

The time slipped by, and everyone remained quiet. Finally, Lord Kentato strode across the courtyard, his men following behind him. They looked the same as before, but there was a change in the way they walked. All of them seemed excited, joyous even. They returned to the field and Master Satoshi looked at Lord Ishida.

"Commander," he said, bowing.

Lailani found it curious that he hadn't bowed to Lord Kentato. Was Lord Ishida of a higher rank somehow? The commander entered through the gates, and Lailani joined the men streaming in behind him. She walked in step with Kalea and Huou. Awe fell over her as she surveyed the details of the school grounds.

Stone posts and lintels supported large wooden-shingled roofs that curved gently upward, giving the buildings a graceful appearance. Orange and brown terracotta statues of faceless warriors stood guard around the primary school building. Despite their lack of facial features, they exuded power and stability. Lailani tore her gaze from them and saw they were heading around the eastern side of the school.

A massive hole in the ground served as the entrance into the underground stable. Lord Ishida didn't pause or hesitate. He walked down the sloping ingress and disappeared into the darkness below. Lailani and the others followed him blindly, not knowing what awaited them. She thought of the excitement Lord Kentato's men displayed. There couldn't be anything ill down here.

*Daigo?*

She tried calling out to the dragon again. A faint impression at the edge of her mind pulled at her. It was a dragon, that much was clear, but it wasn't Daigo. She ignored the pull and descended into the blackness of the tunnel. It wasn't completely dark. Torches flickered along the walls, providing a modicum of light, and she could make out the murky silhouettes of caves. The scent of wet earth wafted into her nostrils, overpowering the smell of her companions.

The rustling of wings and talons scratching on stone alerted them to the presence of the dragons. Here and there, men stepped away from the group and headed into the caves. Lailani tried to keep herself calm. Diago had to be down here somewhere. Unless they had caught him.

*No,* she told herself. *He's fine. I just need to find him.*

Still, it bothered her he wasn't responding. The impression at the edge of her mind grew stronger, more insistent. There was a dragon that wanted her to come to it. Again, she ignored its pull. It could be an untamed one, trying to coax her into being its meal. She would not allow the distraction.

*Daigo. Where are you?*

Most everyone had branched off into a cave, and she was one of only a handful still walking along the tunnel. The insistent pull pounded in her mind like someone beating on a door. And then it abruptly stopped. Lailani paused, glancing to her left. A flash of blue flickered in the darkness of a cave.

*Daigo?*

She stepped across the cave's threshold and listened intently. The heavy breathing of something enormous echoed off the walls. She stepped further into the darkness and saw two eyes staring at her. Reaching her right hand out, she drew hesitantly closer. Why wasn't he answering her?

Her hand touched the dragon's scales. They were hard and smooth. The realization that the dragon wasn't Daigo crossed her mind, but before she could retreat, a warmth spread from her palm outward, rolling throughout her entire body. It wasn't painful. It was … comforting.

*Ameratsu.*

The name flashed through Lailani's mind and she staggered back, pressing her palm to her chest. What was that? Had a dragon just … no, it couldn't have. She was a woman, and no dragon would bond with a woman.

*Daigo!* She screamed his name with all her might.

*Little one? What's wrong?* His words were sluggish, as if he'd just woken.

*Where are you?*

She backed out of the cave and fled further into the tunnel. There were no torches this far down, and she continued blindly ahead until she ran into an immovable object that she thought was a boulder.

*Little one,* Daigo said, sniffing her hair. *What are you doing here?*

She traced her hands on the object and realized it was Daigo's leg.

*You scared me,* she said, unable to stop the tears. She sobbed, wrapping her arms around his neck. *We're here for the bonding ceremony and you weren't answering. I thought ...*

*Forgive me. I was asleep and did not hear you. The bonding ceremony is today? Did I sleep for a week?*

*No, they did it early. I think they are preparing to send us to war.*

L AILANI REMAINED IN the darkness with Daigo until Lord Ishida called for them to leave. She rose to her feet hesitantly, not wanting to leave his side. It had only been a few days since she'd arrived at the camp, and she was already overwhelmed and ready to give up. Protecting her father was the only thing that kept her from doing so.

*Your dragon training should begin soon,* Daigo said. *They can't send you into battle without knowing how to ride.*

*I haven't even learned how to use a weapon. Not fully, anyway. Someone died today during training. I can't help but wonder what if that had been me?*

*It will take time for you to master weapons, but I am confident you will excel with them. Your father was quite skilled with the sword. I'm sure you will have the same skill.*

*I pray I do. I should go, but I don't want to.*

*All will be well. Now that the ceremony is done, we can see each other more frequently and no one will find it suspicious.*

Lailani was glad to hear that. She patted Daigo blindly and carefully walked along the tunnel, heading back the way she'd come. As she passed the cave that held the dragon she'd touched, she could feel the dragon's presence in her mind. It was much different from when she and Daigo mind-spoke, and she remembered Shimura saying it could feel invasive. He was right. Every thought seemed to be drawn to the dragon.

*We are connected, no matter how much you try to ignore the bond.*

The dragon's voice was soft but powerful. It was a female. Ameratsu, if she recalled the name correctly. Lailani ignored the dragon and continued through the tunnel, stepping back into the daylight. She joined the other clan members and followed them through the courtyard and back into the field.

Lord Hisamatsu and his clan entered the school grounds next. Voices rose in excited whispers, and Lailani caught bits and pieces of how the experience went for some of them. Kalea and Huou were next to her, sharing in the excitement.

"A blue dragon," Kalea said, a wide grin pulling at his lips. "Just as I'd hoped. Is yours green?"

"No, it's black. But I'm not upset. The privilege of bonding with a dragon alone is a great honor."

"What about you, Lai? Did you bond with a blue?"

The sight of blue scales flashed in her mind, but she pushed it aside, imagining Daigo's sapphire color.

"Yes."

Their excitement was nice to see, but Lailani was uneasy. Ameratsu said they were bonded, but that couldn't be true, could it? No dragon would bond with a woman, not when the punishment was death. Should she tell Daigo? No. It was better to keep it a secret. The bond couldn't grow if she ignored it.

After Lord Hisamatsu's clan came back from the stable, all three clans returned to the camp. They gathered around the pyre that held Seto's body, and Lord Ishida used a torch to light it on fire. The flames spread quickly, devouring the straw and wood, and eventually Seto's body as well. The atmosphere of the camp was solemn, and once Seto's remains turned to ash and the sun had set, the feast began.

Fireworks boomed in the sky, the white explosions a myriad of shapes and sizes. Food was brought to the meal rug, which was now lined with braziers, and everything from rice and seaweed to roasted meats was laid out. Lailani partook of it all, hoping to drown her worries and forget about Ameratsu. Lord Ishida surprised his clan by bringing several earthen vessels of awamori out, an alcohol made from long grain rice. Once the awamori flowed, everything became more jovial.

Lailani indulged in the alcohol as well, though she didn't drink much. Her father had once told her 'drunk men tell no lies,' and she didn't want to risk revealing her secret because she'd lost her inhibitions. Despite that, the drink gave her a lightlessness that felt good. She enjoyed the festivities, what few were allotted in the military camp, and eventually inched closer to Lord Ishida.

The commander stood at the edge of the meal rug, watching his soldiers enjoy themselves. His expression was smooth and unreadable like stone, but there was something about him that Lailani found intriguing. Alluring, even. Perhaps it had been his kindness on her first day, or perhaps it was the unexplainable attraction she felt toward him.

"Having fun, my Lord?"

He kept his head straight, but his eyes flicked over at her.

"I think you are all having plenty to compensate for my lack of participation."

"Don't you want to loosen up? You're always so serious-looking. We should all be celebrating, shouldn't we? You are our commander, after all. Now that we've bonded with our dragons, we just have to learn to fight and the rest will work itself out."

Her words flowed freely, like a river with no dam. Why was she speaking in such a manner? She'd only had a single cup of awamori. Or was it two? Wait, no. It was three. Maybe. She grinned at him, earning a slight smile from Lord Ishida before his usual impassive mask replaced it.

"Tell me about yourself, Lai."

"What do you want to know, my Lord?"

"Anything." He paused. "Everything."

Her face flushed with warmth, though whether it was from the alcohol or being in his proximity, she didn't know. Was his question innocent, or was he digging for something? She turned her gaze on Kalea and watched him and a few other men laugh and tell stories.

"I'm from an island off the coast. My father was a rider before he retired. I came in his stead when the emperor's decree was issued to save him from dying."

"How noble of you. Most riders die in the service of the empire. How did your father earn a retirement?"

"He has an illness of the body that worsened to the point he could no longer swing a sword or ride his dragon. Since he wasn't fit for battle, he was honorably dismissed."

Lailani became aware of Lord Ishida's eyes on her. She met his stare and held it.

"I'm sorry to hear that," he said. "You bring honor to him by sacrificing yourself on his behalf."

"You speak as though I'm guaranteed to die."

"These are uncertain times. Our days in this life are never guaranteed."

His serious words were hindering her ability to enjoy herself.

"I told you my story. What's yours?"

"You don't want to hear about me," Lord Ishida replied.

"I do."

Something stirred in his eyes.

"Come with me," he said. "I have a stronger drink in my tent."

Lailani walked with him to his pavilion and followed him inside. Paper lanterns were placed at strategic points in the pavilion, offering an even amount of light throughout. It still bothered her that she'd stolen clothes from him. She cast her eyes down at her trousers, a wave of embarrassment washing over her.

"My father served the emperor, and his father before him," Lord Ishida said.

"The emperor must be long-lived."

"No more than any other man."

He grabbed a crystal vase from his desk and poured a pale green liquid into two wooden cups.

"Did your father die at an early age?"

"My father still lives, but he no longer serves the emperor. Not directly, anyway. Here, try this."

He handed her one of the cups. She brought it to her nose and sniffed it. A nutty caramel smell graced her senses, and she took a sip. It was mildly sweet and rolled down her throat easily.

"That's delicious," she said.

"It was a gift from the emperor."

"He must favor you."

Lord Ishida shrugged. "It is difficult to tell some days. His emotions are as unpredictable as a storm. I think my father's fall from grace has left an unpleasant taste in his mouth when it comes to my family."

"What do you mean?"

Lord Ishida stared at her. It was hot in his tent, and the alcohol burning in her throat made it worse. Her armor chafed her, but she dared not be so bold as to take it off. It helped hide her feminine form, not that there was much to her chest.

"My father was once a great general, commanding an entire garrison of troops. When he lost the emperor's favor, he was made a slave."

The description of his father sounded a lot like Mahiro's story. Her eyes widened in realization.

"Your father is Mahiro?"

"How did you know?"

"It was a guess. I trained with him yesterday and he told me the same story. I am sorry your father has lost his honor."

"He didn't lose his honor!" Lord Ishida snapped angrily.

Lailani drew back, startled.

"Forgive me. It is a sensitive matter. I don't like talking about it."

That was obvious. She drank the rest of the liquid and offered her empty cup to him.

"I should get back out there," Lailani said.

"You will stay. For now."

He refilled her cup and motioned her over to the table that held a map of Terran. His outburst made her uncomfortable, but he was her commander. Unless she wanted to be punished, she knew she should obey his orders. She joined him at the table and accepted the cup from him.

"You remind me of myself in some ways. I never intended to follow in my father's footsteps. I wanted to be a scholar, and I could have been, too, if it wasn't for my father's falling out with the emperor."

"You were forced into the military?"

Lord Ishida nodded. "There is no denying the emperor unless you want to find yourself waking up in the afterlife."

"That sounds terrible."

"It is the way of things."

Lord Ishida took a sip from his cup and Lailani could tell by the glow in his eyes that he enjoyed the sweet drink.

"The empire is like a serpent. If you do not learn to navigate around it correctly, it will devour you."

Lailani was losing control of her body. The sweet drink was mixing with the awamori she'd consumed, making her dizzy. She wavered on her feet and thought she was going to fall, but Lord Ishida rested a hand on her arm, steadying her.

"There are few who can hold their alcohol well," he said, offering a chuckle.

It was the first time she heard him laugh. It was a lovely sound. She stared at him, her breath quickening. He was handsome, undeniably so, but she knew nothing could ever happen between them. She was pretending to be a man. If he found out she was something otherwise, he would kill her.

Despite that, she moved closer to him. He watched her intently, but she couldn't read his expression. Could he tell what she desired to do? She closed the distance and pressed her lips to his, kissing him. He returned the gesture with twice the passion, and she wrapped her arms around his neck, pulling him closer.

*Ameratsu.*

The dragon's voice in her mind startled her, and she broke away from Lord Ishida. Clarity struck her and her eyes widened. She had just kissed her commander!

"F-forgive me, my Lord," she stuttered, dropping to her knees. "I don't know what I was thinking."

"Rise," he commanded.

She did so, but she kept her gaze on the floor.

"Look at me."

Again, she obeyed.

"It's fine. I know your secret."

Fear enveloped her, and it must have been clear on her face.

"Do not worry," he said softly. "I will not say anything."

"T-thank you, my Lord. I-I must go."

Lailani turned and fled from the pavilion, rushing across the camp and into her tent. What had she done?

16

IN THE MORNING, Lailani awoke to the pounding of the worst headache she could remember. It was like the beating of drums inside her skull. Her mouth was dry as though full of cotton, and she was disoriented. She sat up, and the tent walls spun around her. Where was she? She caught a flash of Kalea's face before she staggered to the entrance and vomited on the ground.

She remained on her hands and knees until the ground stopped tilting, then returned to her bed with a groan.

"Rough morning?" Huou asked, chuckling.

The sound of his laugh grated on her nerves, but she bit her tongue. It wasn't his fault she'd overindulged last night.

"I don't know why anyone drinks alcohol when this is what the aftereffect is like," she said.

"People enjoy being tortured when it's on their own terms," Kalea chimed in.

Lailani watched them both rise from their bedrolls. They put their armor on and were preparing to leave the tent.

"Don't tell me we still have to train today?"

"You didn't think you got to sleep all day, did you? Yes, we have to train, but we get to spend the day with our dragons."

That was good news, but she still felt like death was waiting to take her to the afterlife. The two men left the tent, leaving her alone. She rolled onto her side and wondered if it was possible to die from drinking whatever Lord Ishida had given her.

Lord Ishida.

The memory of the night before came to the forefront of her mind, and her eyes widened. He knew she was a woman! He said he wouldn't say anything, but why not? Did he feel the same attraction she did toward him? Perhaps he did. There was nothing for him to gain by keeping her secret. It wasn't as if she was from wealth, so he couldn't extort her family.

They had kissed, too. Her cheeks burned, and she eased herself up into a sitting position. Would things be awkward between them now? Should she avoid him? Did he remember what happened, or was the moment lost to the void of drunkenness?

*Ameratsu.*

The dragon's name echoed in her thoughts. She tried to ignore the creature, but its presence lingered in her mind, much like the scent of the powdered incense from Lord Ishida's pavilion wouldn't leave her nostrils. She decided to put him out of her thoughts. War loomed on the horizon, and romance would only distract her from her course.

Lailani forced herself off the bedroll and retrieved one of the sea sponges from the bag hidden underneath it, stuffing the sponge under her cuirass. She'd passed out with her boots and armor on, so she only had to smooth her hair, and then she was on her way through the camp to find a private spot. She performed her ablutions and went to the meal rug, opting to skip breakfast. Her stomach felt too weak to eat anything.

The general atmosphere among the other men was much the same as her own. It was a sea of pale faces, and a few people looked as if they were about to be sick. She didn't foresee much training being accomplished today. Shimura joined them at his usual time and ordered them all to the field.

A host of dragons were waiting for them. Lailani's eyes widened when she saw the vast array of colors gathered. Blues, greens, reds, and even a few black dragons interspersed throughout the tall grass. Lailani was excited to see Daigo and rushed to him.

*Little one. You look ill. Is everything all right?*

*I'm fine,* she replied. *My commander knows I'm a woman.*

*How?*

*His dragon must have told him. He told me he wouldn't say anything.*

*Do you believe him?*

Lailani hesitated. *Yes, I think so.*

She swallowed hard and debated how much to tell him. The kiss was a private matter and telling Daigo felt like it might be a betrayal. If Lord Ishida was going to keep her secret, then she wouldn't tell anyone about their kiss. Ameratsu was another matter. Lailani suspected she was bound to her.

*If you believe him, then we should trust him. For now. If either of us senses trouble from him, we'll flee.*

*Where would we go? We can't return to the Perched Cay.*

*Peace, little one. There doesn't seem to be anything to worry about yet. We'll continue ahead as planned, but we need to be ready to change paths. I don't want to die unless it's in battle.*

*Are you having second thoughts about this?* Lailani asked.

*No. Our agreement still stands, but I've had time to think. I will not die at the hands of the empire unless there's no other way.*

Lailani didn't disagree with him. She wanted to live a long life after all of this was over. She decided not to tell him about Ameratsu for now. They spent the rest of the day learning about their dragons. Proper saddling techniques, a flight over the school grounds, and a brief discourse from Master Satoshi about how to strengthen the bond.

Although the latter part wasn't pertinent to her, Lailani still paid attention and tried to commit what she heard to memory in case they were tested on it later. As the hours passed, the sick feeling in her stomach went away and her headache faded. Lunch was a quick affair, and then they went back to training.

While they were working through saddling their dragons, Lord Ishida joined them on the field. He stopped and spoke with each soldier, asking questions and looking over the dragons. When he got to Lailani, he stared at her dragon for a long while without speaking.

"M-my lord," she greeted, breaking the silence.

"Something isn't right. This dragon is old and battle-scarred. He should not have been in the caves. Did you seal the bond with him?"

*He's a funny one staring at me,* Daigo said.

"Yes, the bond is sealed. I am pleased with him, my Lord. His scars are a sign of his prowess and experience. I am honored to have him."

Lord Ishida turned his gaze on her. The memory of their kiss made her knees go weak, but she locked them in place and did her best to seem unbothered by his presence. He flicked his eyes along her frame and turned away, walking to the next rider. Lailani heaved a sigh of relief.

*You like him.*

*What? No, I—h-he's just intimidating.*

Daigo laughed. *If you say so, little one.*

The rest of the day was uneventful, and Lailani was glad for the time spent with her father's dragon. She was accustomed to flying, but using a saddle took some getting used to. The dragons returned to the stable under the school, and Shimura dismissed the men for the evening.

Lailani met with Mahiro in the field near the camp at dusk and they went through more *bujutsu* exercises. She remembered a few of the movements from the other night, but most of it seemed new. The knowledge that Mahiro was Lord Ishida's father was difficult to wrap her mind around, since the two didn't resemble one another at all. That the emperor forced Mahiro to be a slave and serve under his own son was appalling. Daigo had been right. The world truly was a monstrous place.

After she completed her lesson, Lailani returned to her tent and tiredly removed her armor. Kalea and Huou were still awake, and they invited her to join in their conversation. She was so exhausted her eyes were closing of their own volition, so she surrendered to sleep. Her dreams were full of odd places and tormented images, and at one point she woke up drenched in sweat.

There was no doubt in her mind that the bond with Ameratsu was the cause of her nightmares. She would have to work harder to keep the dragon out of her mind, make it a habit so that it did not affect her while she slept. Perhaps Daigo could help her with that if she found a clever way to glean the information.

When the sun rose, Lailani rolled out of bed and got ready, then went to the field to practice her *bujutsu* form sequences. Lord Ishida might know she was a woman, but she didn't want him to think that meant she couldn't be a warrior. He'd questioned her choice with Daigo, which told her he had his doubts.

She would prove to him she wasn't helpless. She would prove it to everyone.

OVER THE NEXT week, the whispers of an impending call to the front lines died down. Their training schedule was split, with the morning hours being devoted to sparring under Shimura's watchful eye while they spent the afternoon with their dragons. Master Satoshi spent time with them daily, giving guidance and advice on how to handle the massive creatures.

For Lailani, there was no respite. From sunrise until the moon shone above, she worked herself harder than ever before. She learned to wield a sword beyond clumsy swings, and with Daigo's instruction, flying became second nature. At the end of each day, despite her exhaustion, she practiced the *bujutsu* movements.

It didn't take long for her to realize the things Mahiro taught her could also apply to life and working with dragons. Perhaps that was why, of all twelve forms, he chose to teach her the Dragon.

Today, they were going to take turns flying past the boundaries of the school to perform faux scout missions. They were being sent as trios, and Lailani was eager to see who would be placed with her. She watched Kalea as he traversed the field, pausing near each clan member to give instruction. He didn't let the power of being a Talon Leader go to his head, and he treated everyone with dignity and respect.

The sun shined hot, causing sweat to collect in places Lailani would rather not think about. She brushed the back of her hand across her brow as Kalea approached.

"You're with me," he said. "Who should our third be?"

"I assumed you'd pick Huou," she replied.

"I considered it, but I need him to keep an eye on Kento and Yugi. They've been acting out, so I assigned him to their group. Maybe he can rub off on them and help them mature."

Lailani nodded. Those two were the youngest in the camp, so their antics did not surprise her. She scanned the field and settled her eyes on the disgraced general.

"Let's take Mahiro."

"We can't. He doesn't have a dragon."

"He can ride with one of us."

"No. He's not allowed to leave the camp without Lord Ishida's permission, and I don't foresee him granting the request. Any other suggestions?"

Lailani shrugged. "No."

"Then we'll take Kenji."

She stiffened at the warrior monk's name. Ever since he'd broken her leg on the first day of training, she'd kept her distance from him. He wasn't mean, and she knew he hadn't injured her intentionally, but her fear of the man was strong. Perhaps this would be an opportunity to get past that fear.

"Good choice," she said.

"Get ready, then. We're going first." He pointed northeast. "There's not much to see that way, but the terrain will give us plenty to scout out."

Kalea strode over to Kenji to deliver the news, then headed toward his dragon. Lailani climbed into the saddle on Daigo's back, shifting until she was comfortably seated.

*I like him,* Daigo said.

*He's always been a good friend to me back on the island. It is nice to see that even with a rise in rank, he remains the same man.*

The dragon rumbled in agreement.

Daigo waited until Kalea's dragon was airborne, then launched himself skyward and followed after the Talon Leader. A few moments later, Kenji and his dragon joined them and together they flew over the camp, heading in the direction Kalea had indicated. The air pulled at Lailani, and she hunched lower, shielding her eyes with her right arm while keeping a tight hold on the saddle horn with her left.

The one thing she didn't like about flying was the way her eyes dried out. If she kept them closed, she couldn't enjoy the view, but if she kept them open, the wind irritated them to the point of pain. She'd found that using her arm to block the wind helped, but it partially obscured her view and wouldn't be feasible if she were in a battle.

*Why doesn't the wind bother you?* She asked Daigo.

*We dragons have two eyelids. You can see one of them, but the other is clear and invisible to you. It protects my vision.*

*I wish I had something like that.*

*Perhaps humans aren't meant to fly.*

*Then why are we able to bond with dragons?*

*That's the age-old question,* Daigo laughed.

They flew for half an hour before Kalea motioned for them to break formation. The previous day, Shimura had led them in a similar exercise. She and Daigo excelled, but that was because he'd done this all before. Their progress impressed the captain, and he congratulated her. It wasn't much, but it bolstered her confidence.

Daigo veered to the left while Kalea continued straight. Kenji went to the right. His dragon was green like Huou's, and she watched its sinuous body undulate through the sky. She'd heard some of the other men say that there were dragons in Osnen that had wings. Wings! What kind of dragon had wings? If that were true, they probably looked odd.

*Look down at our left,* Daigo said, shattering her thoughts.

She did as he asked and saw a long river that snaked along the landscape. It glistened under the sunlight, bright patches of white light reflecting up at her.

*It's beautiful.*

*When it rains in the mountains, the water flows down and fills the river until it overflows. The land here is uninhabitable because of that. The floods make it too dangerous.*

It occurred to her that the most beautiful things often posed the greatest danger. She watched the scenery pass as Daigo glided at a casual pace. Woods swallowed the river the further they went, and she spotted a doe and her babies on the edge of the tree line. They sprinted for cover when Daigo's shadow fell over them.

*If this were a real scouting assignment, what would we be looking for? Enemies?*

*Anything out of the ordinary. Enemies are less likely to be seen in the open, but they can make mistakes. My eyes are better suited to see from this distance than yours, but you may catch something I miss.*

*Do the Roarans have dragons?*

*No.*

*Then I don't understand how the imperial army can be losing.*

*The Roarans may not have dragons, but they do have sorcerers.*

*But dragons have magic, which makes them more powerful, right?*

*Not always.*

*What do you mean?* Lailani asked.

*Some sorcerers are more powerful than dragons. They are few, but they are out there in the world. I suspect there may be some in the Roarans ranks. That would explain the heavy losses the army is sustaining.*

It was difficult for her to fathom a human defeating a dragon. Dragons were massive and the most powerful creatures in the world. At least, that's what she had believed all this time. If a sorcerer could overpower a dragon, what else could they do?

Amid the forest, she saw a break in the canopy. It didn't look natural.

*Look there,* she said, pointing. *There's a dark spot in the woods. What is it?*

*Let us get closer to investigate.*

Daigo changed course and descended slowly. They flew over the break and Lailani glimpsed a flash of red. Was that a dragon?

*Fly over it again. I think I saw something.*

*You did see something. I saw it, too, but I can't tell if she's injured.*

Daigo wheeled around and returned to the break in the canopy. He flew in place, hovering over the hole. Lailani peered around his neck and saw a red dragon on the ground. It wasn't moving.

*Can you land down there?*

*Not easily.*

Daigo swiveled his head from side to side. *I can land at the edge of the woods. You'll have to go on foot.*

*No. Lower me down from here.*

Lailani thought he was going to argue with her. Instead, he twisted his body, angling his tail down into the canopy. Lailani slid down his curved form, her tiny fingers digging between his scales for purchase. When she reached his tail, the scales were too closely knitted to find crevices, so she wrapped her arms around him tightly and slid down, little by little.

She slipped and fell, crashing to the hard ground roughly and bashing her head. Pain exploded behind her eyes and she gasped. It took a moment to get her bearings, but she finally managed to stand and blink the tears from her eyes.

The body of a long red dragon stretched out before her. It was completely still, and she gently placed a hand on its side. It wasn't breathing.

*I think she's dead.*

*Do you see anyone with her?*

Lailani walked along the creature's length and saw she was wearing a saddle. Not wanting to climb over the dragon and desecrate the body, she went around to the other side, passing by its head. The dragon's lifeless gaze stared off into the distance, dried blood on the corners of her mouth. She frowned, saddened by the dragon's death. It was still beautiful, though, even in death.

Her eyes trailed down the creature's body. She didn't see any wounds or blood aside from what was on its mouth. Moving slowly toward the saddle, she froze, eyes wide.

*There's a body.*

A RIDER WEARING the colors of the imperial army was lying on the ground, his legs pinned under the dragon. His eyes were closed, but his chest moved with his breathing.

*He's alive,* she said, kneeling beside him.

*Is he from the school?*

*No. He's an imperial.*

*He's probably a messenger. We need to get him back to the camp. Can you carry him?*

*I can't move him. He's stuck under the dragon. I need help.*

*I'll get the others.*

Daigo left. With his bulk gone, the clearing filled with sunlight. Lailani surveyed the area and noticed damage to the trees. It was obvious the dragon had fallen from the sky, but had something attacked the dragon, or had she fallen mid-flight from exhaustion?

The rider had several nicks and scratches, but she didn't see any major injuries. His legs could be broken, so they would need to move him carefully. She slid his helmet off and ran her fingers gently across his cheek. The soldier's eyes fluttered open.

"We're going to get you out of here," Lailani said.

"Shojin Mountains," he whispered.

"What?"

His eyes rolled into the back of his head and he went unconscious. She frowned. Why did he say that? And what did it mean? They needed to get him back to the camp, and quickly. She stood and looked around the clearing. Broken tree limbs littered the ground. A few of them looked long and thick enough to hold the soldier's weight, so she collected them and set them in place near him.

She needed something to tie them together. The saddle's straps offered a simple solution. Lailani stepped over to the dragon and placed a hand on her cold scales.

"Forgive me," she whispered.

Lailani drew her sword and cut the straps from the saddle and used them to bind the branches, creating a makeshift litter. Once she pulled the man out from under the dragon, she'd be able to carry him out of the woods.

She looked up when she heard someone approaching. It was Kenji. Fear threatened to overtake her, but she clenched her jaw and pushed through the feeling. He was an ally, not an enemy.

"He's over here," she said, waving her arm.

The warrior monk joined her and took in the sight. He walked over to the dragon and tried to push her bulk off the man, but he may as well have tried to move a mountain. Kenji stepped back and grunted.

"One of the dragons will have to lift her."

"Where's your dragon?" Lailani asked.

"At the far end of the woods."

Daigo reappeared over the clearing.

"I'll ask mine to move her." She paused and stared at the prone soldier. "He woke up for a moment."

"Did he say anything?"

"Only two words. Shojin Mountains. Does that mean anything to you?"

"It's the range at the northern tip of Terran. The monastery where I trained is there."

"Is there anything else there? Why would that be the only thing he could think of?"

"I do not know."

Lailani looked up at Daigo. *Can you lift her?*

*Yes.*

He lowered his back end through the canopy and grabbed onto the dragon with his rear claws. Lailani didn't want to disrespect the creature, but it was the only way to get the soldier free. Daigo heaved upward and Kenji pulled the man onto the litter.

*It's clear,* Lailani said.

Daigo lowered the dragon back down.

*I will meet you at the edge of the woods.*

He left, and Lailani helped Kenji lift the litter. It was wobbly, but the saddle straps held. They trekked through the woods, heading in the direction that Kenji had come from. When they cleared the trees, all three dragons and Kalea were waiting for them.

"Let's put him on your dragon," Kalea said to Lailani. "Kenji, you head back to the camp and inform Lord Ishida what we've found. Tell him to have his healer ready."

The three of them worked together to get the litter onto Daigo's back, setting it behind the saddle. Lailani was worried it was going to fall off in flight, so Kalea used a small portion of the straps to secure it to the saddle. It wasn't ideal, but it was better than before. Kenji mounted his dragon and departed for the camp.

"I would take him on mine, but he's still adjusting to having a rider. Your dragon is the best suited for this task."

"We'll be careful," she replied.

"I'll fly behind you and keep an eye on him, as well as on our surroundings. I don't know what happened, but I don't like this."

Kalea looked to the sky and scanned the horizon.

"We should hurry. He could have internal injuries and there's nothing we can do for him."

"Yes, sir," Lailani said.

She hurried into the saddle and Daigo took off. Lailani continuously looked back to check on the man. He didn't move at all, and the straps holding the litter to her saddle remained firm. When they reached the field outside the camp, Lord Ishida and Shimura were waiting with Lady Narumi and a few other soldiers.

Daigo spiraled down, landing gently among the tall grass, and the soldiers quickly brought the litter down and carried the man to the camp, Lady Narumi walking with them.

"My Lord," Lailani greeted.

"Tell me everything."

"We were scouting the terrain when I saw a hole in the canopy of the woods. Further inspection revealed a dragon."

"Where is it?"

"She's dead. I think she fell from the sky."

"What of the rider? Has he been unconscious this whole time?"

"Yes, mostly. He awoke once and said 'Shojin Mountains.' Neither Kenji nor I know what he meant."

"Clear the field and leave us," Lord Ishida said, looking at Shimura. The captain bowed and ordered Kalea and those who remained to head back to the camp. The dragons, all except Daigo, left for the school's stables.

Lord Ishida looked at Daigo. "Return to the stable."

Daigo didn't budge.

"Is the beast deaf?" he asked heatedly, turning to Lailani. "I gave him an order."

"Yes, my Lord. He is deaf."

Lord Ishida's serious demeanor turned to surprise.

"What?"

Lailani swallowed hard. "My dragon is deaf. He can only hear words in his mind or feel vibrations."

An awkward silence ensued, and Lailani cast her eyes to the ground. Now he knew another of her secrets.

"A beast like him should never have been among the others. If you weren't bound to him already, I'd have him removed. Why didn't you say anything earlier?"

"Until now, did you suspect he couldn't hear?"

Lord Ishida scowled. "No."

"He appeared fit to serve the empire, yes? That's because he is. His deafness does not make him less than any other. He has been deaf for many years and has learned to navigate life without sound."

"He's going to get you killed."

"I respectfully disagree, my Lord."

They stared one another in the eyes for a moment, then Lord Ishida sighed.

"Did the messenger say anything else?"

"No. He lost consciousness again after he mentioned the mountains."

"Do not speak of this to anyone."

"I've not told anyone but you about Daigo's impairment, my Lord."

"Not that," Lord Ishida said. "If anyone asks, the messenger has not awoken at all. I'll have Shimura tell Kenji the same thing."

"Is something wrong?"

"That remains to be seen. Tell your dragon to go to the stable and get yourself back to camp."

He turned and strode off briskly.

Lailani looked at Daigo.

*He knows.*

*It was only a matter of time, little one. At least he didn't expel me. Or you.*

Lailani wondered at that, but she suspected it had something to do with what they shared on the night of the bonding ceremony.

*I'll see you tomorrow. Hopefully, we'll have some answers by then.*

Daigo exhaled through his nose, ruffling her hair. She smiled and walked back to the camp. Rumors were already being spread among the men. Some said the messenger had been attacked while others said something out there was preying on dragons. Lailani believed it was the former, but there was no evidence to prove it.

She stopped at the water trough to drink, then went to her tent. The more she considered the idea of an attack on the rider, the more she grew troubled. Had the Roarans defeated the imperial army? Had they invaded Terran already? She supposed they would have already received word of such a defeat, from displaced villagers, if no one else.

With any luck, Lady Narumi would heal the man and he would deliver his message—and reveal what happened to his dragon. Maybe she was overthinking things. Perhaps the dragon had died from normal causes and she was allowing her subconscious fears to dwell in her mind.

Yes, that was it. Soon they would have an answer, and it would put her mind at ease.

TRAINING RESUMED THE next day as normal, with multiple patrols being sent to the area where the messenger had been found. A team of riders pulled the dead dragon from the woods, whose dragons did all the work, and they laid her to rest by setting her ablaze.

None of the patrols found any signs of what caused the dragon's death, but everyone remained alert and the school sent scouts further out to ensure there wasn't trouble brewing. At the camp, Lady Narumi treated the messenger and healed his wounds, confirming that he miraculously hadn't sustained internal damage. Despite her treatment, he remained unconscious for another full day.

Lord Ishida kept the man in his pavilion, and when word got out that he was awake, the camp erupted in more rumors. Kalea and the other Talon Leaders reported to the pavilion at Shimura's command and everyone else waited eagerly for details. When Kalea returned, his expression told Lailani that they were about to receive bad news. He, along with the other Talon Leaders, gathered their clan members together.

"The messenger was sent by the emperor," Kalea said.

"What happened to his dragon?" Huou asked.

"A spell injured her before leaving the front lines. It took its toll on her and she collapsed. Thankfully, the rider survived the fall, otherwise we wouldn't know how dire the situation is at the border."

Lailani felt bad for the man. It was said that losing the bond was akin to dying yourself. Some never recovered from the loss, and those who did were never the same.

"What's happening at the border?" someone asked.

"The imperial line of defense is crumbling. Lord Kentato and Lord Hisamatsu have been called to the front lines as reinforcements."

Lailani held her breath. What of them? If they weren't going to the front lines, what was their assignment?

"You may have heard that the messenger mentioned the Shojin Mountains. The Roarans have sent a force of men through the Shingtai Pass intending to circle around to strike at the imperial army from behind, trapping them. The emperor has ordered Lord Ishida to stop that force at all costs."

He paused, looking at everyone. "We leave within the hour."

"What are we supposed to do? We've barely been trained for battle."

"We're all the emperor has," Kalea told the man. "If we don't stop them, the empire will fall."

"We can't allow that," Lailani said. "Think of our families. If the Roarans are free to traverse Terran, they will kill everyone and burn all in their path. We may not have much training, but that doesn't mean we can't defeat them. We have the might of our dragons with us."

"Lai is right. Some of us came here in our fathers' stead. We've wasted our effort if we do not step up when we're needed. I will also remind you all that if you abandon your post, Lord Ishida will bring you to justice."

"Not if he's dead like the rest of us," someone muttered.

"Who said that?" Kalea demanded.

No one spoke.

"Armor up and meet me in the school's courtyard."

The men scattered. Lailani rested her hand on the hilt of her sword and glanced around the camp. Her only belongings were the clothes she was wearing and her armor, and she had stolen the clothes. She stared at Lord Ishida's pavilion.

This was it. They were going to join the war. He knew she was a woman, and yet he was going to allow her the honor of fighting in her father's place.

Lord Ishida was a good man and a good leader. He was willing to keep her secrets at the peril of losing his own life, just like Daigo.

The feelings she experienced when she was around him were confusing, but they felt … right. Maybe after the war was over, if they won, something might blossom between them, but until then … Lailani tightened her grip on the hilt. Until that time, she was no longer Lailani. She was Lai.

She left the camp and marched across the field to the school. With every step, she could feel Ameratsu's presence growing. It was harder to ignore her when she was this close to the dragon, but she fortified the mental wall she'd erected and entered the stable. The tunnels were bustling with riders as they saddled their dragons and began leading them aboveground.

*Daigo,* she called out.

*Little one. What's going on?*

A wave of mental pressure struck Lailani as she walked past Ameratsu's cave and it forced her to lean against the wall.

*Leave me alone,* she told the dragon.

*Ameratsu.*

*What do you want from me?*

*Your name, human. What is your name? I have given you mine. Now give me yours.*

*Why?*

*We are bound, no matter how you try to ignore me.*

*I didn't ask to bond with you.*

*Little one?* It was Daigo. Having two dragons in her head was an odd sensation.

*It's time to go,* Lailani told him. *The emperor needs us at the Shojin Mountains.*

The crunch of dirt signaled his approach, and his head snaked into the light. Lailani walked with him, casting a final glance back over her shoulder at Ameratsu's cave.

*My name is Lailani.*

A satisfied rumble echoed through the tunnel and Lailani pushed the dragon out of her mind. Once they were aboveground, she climbed into the saddle and they joined the other riders in the courtyard. Lord Ishida and Shimura arrived while they waited on a few stragglers, and Lailani saw Mahiro was riding with Lord Ishida.

Father and son, yet brothers in arms.

After everyone was assembled, Lord Ishida raised his hand for silence.

"Given what happened to the messenger, we've lost two days. The Roarans may have already crossed through the Shingtai Pass, but I pray to my ancestors they haven't. I intend to make up the time and get us there as quickly as possible, so we will only stop when it's necessary. Be vigilant and keep your eyes open. The enemy may well be here already."

With that, Lord Ishida took the lead, urging his dragon into the sky. The others followed him, and Lailani turned in the saddle to admire the host of dragons that swarmed into the sky. Their clan had dozens of soldiers, and the rainbow of dragon colors that undulated before her was one of the most beautiful sights she had ever witnessed.

*How can we lose with such a force behind us?* She asked.

*Numbers do not always equate to power. If they did, we would have driven the Roarans to destruction, leaving none behind.*

*This isn't the first time they've attacked?*

*No. Our histories are tangled and bloody. This is the first time the empire has suffered so many losses to them.*

*I wonder what's changed?*

*As do I,* Daigo said.

Their journey across the empire was uneventful. Every city and village they passed was unharmed. It gave Lailani hope the Roarans had not gotten far. Lord Ishida only allowed them to stop a handful of times, mostly to allow the dragons a respite. Meals were sparse and devoured quickly, and the food was always cold. There was no time for fires, no time for rest.

The fate of the empire laid in their hands, and their grip was tenuous at best.

Lailani was exhausted when they made their last stop before reaching the Shingtai Pass. They had flown for hours without sleep, and her lips were dry from the wind. She joined Lord Ishida on the bank of the Mu River to drink. The waterway wound down the Shinjo Mountains and flowed west across the empire, eventually merging into the Sea of Colisle.

The water was freezing, but between her armor and the heat of the sun, it felt good on her hot skin.

"We draw near to danger," Lord Ishida said.

"It seems quiet." Lailani looked up at the mountains. High up the steep slopes, she spotted a few birds of prey circling, probably preparing to eat a dead animal.

"Do not be fooled by the silence. It can hide many things."

There was something she had on her mind, and she stepped closer to him and lowered her voice.

"I want to apologize, my Lord. I should have been honest with you. About everything."

Even as she said those last words, she knew there was still one secret he didn't know about, but she feared if he knew she wasn't bound to Daigo, that would be one too many slights against her.

"There are many traits to be admired, but honesty is the one I value most. If you cannot be honest with me, that means you don't trust me. I have done all I can to ensure there are no barriers between us. If you still don't trust me, I'm not sure that you ever will."

"I do trust you," Lailani said quickly. "I'm just afraid."

"We are all afraid. What matters is how we face our fears."

His words resonated deeply within her. Still, she could not reveal that she and Daigo weren't truly bound. Not because she didn't trust him, but because she knew he would think she was a liar.

"Were the scouts able to tell if the Roarans have already come through the area?"

"It doesn't appear so. The Oshi monastery is near the pass. We will take up a position there and prepare for the arrival of our enemies."

Lailani bowed and left, returning to Daigo's side.

*I smell something foul in the air,* the dragon said.

Lailani inhaled a deep breath, but she didn't smell anything ill.

*What is it?*

*Death.*

THERE WASN'T ENOUGH room in the main plaza to fit them all, so Lord Ishida had them land their dragons on the slopes outside the monastery. They continued on foot, crossing through the first torii, a gate marking the entrance to the monastery. It consisted of two cylindrical posts that rose vertically up out of the ground, topped crosswise with a rectangular beam that extended beyond the posts on both sides. The entire thing was painted bright red, standing in stark contrast to the landscape.

A worn path continued straight to a second torii, followed by another path, though it was shorter than the first. Two stone lion-dog statues, six feet in height, stood on either side of a third torii which led into the plaza, symbolic protectors of the sacred place. Shimura took the lead and stepped into the square, glancing around. He motioned for the rest of the men to follow, and they filed in behind him.

Lailani looked up at the multi-tiered pagoda, admiring its beauty. It had the same design as the school, though this structure was much smaller in comparison. A modest plot of vegetation had been planted on the left side, and on the right side, someone had raked a flat expanse of sand into a swirling design. Other than those sights, the plaza was empty. They stood in silence until Kenji pushed to the front of the group.

"Where is everyone?" Lord Ishida asked.

Shimura looked at Kenji. "Are your brothers in prayer?"

The warrior monk looked up at the sky and shook his head. "It is not time yet."

"Search the place," Lord Ishida instructed.

The soldiers spread out across the plaza, and Kenji went inside the pagoda. Lailani remained where she was and looked back the way they'd come. She couldn't shake the feeling that someone was watching her. A strangled cry came from within the pagoda, and Shimura led a group of soldiers inside. Lailani drew her sword and rushed to the threshold.

Bodies littered the floor. Many of them wore the same head tattoo as Kenji. The warrior monk was on his knees, his shoulders slumped. Even the strongest could become weak. Lailani's heart wrenched for the man. The people he'd grown up with were dead, murdered at the hands of the Roarans.

"Our enemy has already passed through here," Lord Ishida said. "We must find them."

"There was no sign of their passing," Shimura replied. "How will we track them down?"

"We will split into groups and search everywhere."

"My Lord," Shimura lowered his voice. "We are too few to spread ourselves so thin. If the Roarans have made it through the pass, we should stay as one force. If they are expecting us, it will be easier for them to pick us off in smaller groups."

"You are right, but if they *aren't* expecting us, we'll have a better chance of finding them by splitting up."

"Lord Ishida!"

Everyone turned toward the sound of the voice. It was Mahiro. He was in the courtyard, pointing up at the mountainside.

"The enemy is here!"

Whistling filled the air, and a moment later, an arrow struck Mahiro in the shoulder. He toppled backward and Lord Ishida cried out, moving to exit the pagoda. Shimura grabbed onto his arm.

"Stay here, my Lord! They will surely strike you down as well!"

"He needs aid!"

Without thinking, Lailani rushed into the plaza, skidding to a halt beside Mahiro. She pulled him to his feet, careful not to touch his shoulder.

"You fool, now they will kill us both," he grunted.

Arrows *clinked* against the flagstones around them, and one narrowly missed striking Mahiro in the leg. Lailani helped him run to the pagoda. Behind the monastery, at least a dozen men with bows were scattered among the hills. They reached safety, and Lord Ishida's eyes met hers. He offered a nod.

"They're encamped in the hills," she said.

"How many?"

"I'm not sure. I only saw archers."

"We've walked into a trap." Lord Ishida clenched his jaw and looked at his father.

"I'm fine," Mahiro said. "I've had worse wounds."

He grabbed onto the end of the arrow protruding from his shoulder and jerked it free. It had struck perfectly between two of the metal plates of his armor. Blood immediately stained the material. Lady Narumi stepped over to him and gingerly pressed a hand over the wound. She whispered under her breath and pulled her hand away.

"We need to get out of here before they close in," Shimura said.

"The risk is too great," Lord Ishida replied. "Their archers will take many lives before we reach our dragons."

"Then we need to call our dragons here."

There was a moment of silence, and Lord Ishida's eyes widened. "There's something wrong with my bond. I can feel my dragon's presence, but I cannot communicate with her."

The other men muttered their agreement and Lailani grew uneasy. What could block a bond? She tried speaking with Daigo, but he didn't respond. One of her conversations with him came to mind. Some sorcerers were more powerful than dragons. Could it be possible that one of them was among the Roarans?

"We will make our stand here, then," Lord Ishida said, drawing his sword. "The Roarans cannot get past us."

The courage Lailani had when she rushed to Mahiro's aid suddenly fled. The room felt too small. Her throat constricted and she felt suffocated. She forced herself to breathe deeply, and the pounding of her heart eased somewhat. Lord Ishida began issuing orders, but Lailani barely heard his voice. The wave of fear finally subsided, and she noticed Kenji crawling closer to one of the bodies. What was he doing?

The corpse sat up, and Kenji froze. Lailani's eyes widened. The dead had risen! She caught the flash of steel and realized the truth. She screamed a warning, but it was too late. The body drove a dagger into Kenji's throat. The other bodies rose to their feet.

"Dark sorcery!" Shimura shouted.

"No," Lord Ishida said. "A sick ruse. Attack!"

The soldiers rushed forward and clashed with the enemy. Several of Lord Ishida's men fell quickly. Kalea and Huou rushed into the fray, and Lailani joined them. The three of them formed a deadly line of defense and cut down a group of Roarans.

"There!" Huou shouted.

At the back of the room, a figure dressed in black robes was in the middle of spellcasting. Huou broke from their line and rushed forward. One of the Roarans swiftly met him, sword poised over his head.

Huou stepped aside. Their blades met, and the sound of their steel clashing echoed off the walls, adding to the rest of the noise in the room.

As their swords parted, the Roaran soldier aimed a quick cut at Huou's neck. He parried effortlessly and returned the attack in kind. The Roaran caught the slice with his sword and another blade that had sprung to his hand from thin air. One of his blades slid free, barely missing Huou's shoulder.

Huou retreated, slipping in the blood that slicked the lacquered bamboo floor. Cursing, he toppled backward. The Roaran closed in, sword raised for the kill. Huou lashed out with his right foot. The strike connected with the Roaran's left ankle, and the man lurched forward. Huou rolled away from the intended blow and stood. The Roaran warrior caught himself before he fell, turning with a lightning-swift move, and swung his sword in a wide arc. The blade sliced into the back of Huou's knees, in a spot without armor. To his credit, Huou didn't cry out as he dropped to them.

The Roaran retracted his sword and stepped around to face Huou. He thrust the blade into Huou's chest, between the plates of his armor. Lailani screamed and fell to her knees, dropping her sword. Kalea surged ahead, striking the Roaran down before he could turn around. Lailani scrambled to Huou's side on all fours, ignoring the blood that slicked her hands from the floor.

Huou's lifeless gaze stared at the ceiling. Tears stung her eyes. Her friend was dead. She blinked the tears away and rose to her feet, rage replacing anguish. The robed man in the back of the room was still using his magic, oblivious to his surroundings.

Lailani picked up Huou's sword and strode toward the man, her grip tight on the hilt.

She was a few strides away when a shadow to her left detached from the wall and intercepted her. The figure surprised her, and before she could make a move to attack, she felt the cold steel of his sword at her neck.

21

L AILANI SWALLOWED AND the blade bit into her skin. A droplet of blood ran down her neck.

"Drop it," the man ordered.

She released the sword and it fell to the floor with a clang. He whirled her around and wrapped his left arm around her neck, pressing the tip of his sword into her back. Over half of Lord Ishida's men were dead, and those who remained had been subdued, forced onto their knees. More Roarans poured through the doorway into the pagoda and began binding her fellow soldiers.

Kalea was among the living, and she felt some small relief. She'd lost one friend already. Two would be impossible to bear. The man pushed her forward, sending her crashing to the floor. Another Roaran twisted her arms behind her back, binding her wrists with rope. He dragged her over to the others and took up a stance behind her.

The man who intercepted her sheathed his blade and stepped out of the shadows. His hair was long and black, unkempt and wild. Madness was in his green eyes, and a long scar stretched down from his forehead to the right side of his chin.

"Is this what the emperor sent?" His voice was deep and smooth. "A contingent of untrained fools? Which one of you leads this rabble?"

"I do," Lord Ishida answered.

The Roaran walked closer and knelt in front of the commander, tilting his head to the side.

"Why do you try to stop the inevitable? The emperor's forces cannot withstand the Roaran might. Surely you know you are on a fool's errand."

Lord Ishida clenched his jaw, but he didn't say anything. Lailani subtly tried to get free of her bonds, but the rope was too tight.

"I want to know the emperor's plans," the Roaran said. "If one of you can tell me, I will spare your life."

"We will never tell you anything," Lord Ishida said.

"Does one voice speak for the many?"

The Roaran stood and looked down the line of prisoners. No one moved. It surprised Lailani that even in the face of certain death, their loyalty was unyielding.

"Untie me and let us duel," Lord Ishida demanded.

"Do you think I am a fool? Why would I risk my advantage to satisfy your ego?"

"So you are afraid. I *will* kill you before this day ends."

The Roaran laughed. "The fire of your spirit is strong. I like that, though it will not save you. Once my master has killed the emperor, the rest of Terran will fall into line. And if they do not, we will cut them down without compassion. I will offer mercy one final time. Tell me his plans."

No one spoke.

"Very well. If you will not give me what I want willingly, then I will take it by force."

The Roaran leader placed his hand on Lord Ishida's head and closed his eyes. Lailani watched his lips move, but he didn't utter any words. Lord Ishida tensed and his face turned red. His entire body trembled, but the Roaran's hand kept the commander from falling forward. Blood dripped from Lord Ishida's nose, and the Roaran pulled his hand away.

"Your mind is as powerful as your spirit. I'm impressed. Still, one of your soldiers must know something."

Lailani assumed Shimura was the only one who Lord Ishida shared knowledge with, but she knew he would not betray the commander. The Roaran looked among the captives and met Lailani's gaze. He walked over to her and rested his hand on her head.

"We can do this with less pain if you prefer?"

Lailani clenched her jaw and glared at the man. He smiled.

"Stubborn like your commander. No matter. I delight in the pain of others."

Fire tore through her skull. She opened her mouth to scream, but no sound escaped her. Memories flashed before her eyes. Her father helping her catch a fish for the first time. Her mother humming a bedtime tune. The first time she rode on Daigo's back. Her father tending to her sick mother. That memory stung almost as deeply as the Roaran's magic. Tears pooled in her eyes, falling free and landing on the bamboo floor in front of her, mingling with the blood.

More memories flooded past, the images flashing too quickly for her to recognize. Until the last one. The Roaran snatched his hand away and staggered back a step, his face curled in disgust.

"A woman," he hissed.

Lailani felt the invisible weight of dozens of eyes staring at her, both enemy and ally. Or perhaps now they were all enemies. One of Lord Ishida's soldiers had slipped his bonds. He got to his feet and rushed the Roaran leader, tackling him to the ground. Emboldened by the move, the other soldiers, though still bound, also rose to their feet and began kicking at their Roaran captors.

Chaos unfolded in the pagoda, and Lailani rolled to the right, looking for a weapon. Huou's sword still lay at the feet of the sorcerer at the back of the room. She struggled to stand and made a run for it, careful not to slip in the blood that soaked the floor. It was awkward trying to pick up the sword backward, but she propped it against the wall and sliced through the ropes without cutting herself.

She grabbed the hilt and drove the blade into the sorcerer's stomach. Broken from his spellcasting, his pained eyes looked at her in shock. He gasped and fell to his knees, his hands grabbing onto the sword. Lailani watched in horrid fascination until the man slumped lifelessly. She pulled the sword free and ran back to the others, cutting Lord Ishida's bonds.

He snatched a sword from the floor and engaged one of the Roaran soldiers. Lailani turned her attention to freeing more of her companions while blocking swords trying to stab her. Multiple roars overshadowed the sounds of battle, and the pagoda trembled as dragons landed in the courtyard.

*Little one?*

*I'm here,* she told Daigo.

The fighting spilled out of the pagoda and into the courtyard, and the dragons promptly aided their riders by snapping enemy soldiers up in their jaws or swatting them with their tails. Within moments, the tide turned to their favor, and the Roarans were defeated, their bodies scattered about the plaza. Lailani ran across the sand garden to Daigo and wrapped her arms around his leg, dropping her sword to the ground.

*I killed someone,* she said.

*It is difficult to take a life, but sometimes there is no other way.*

Lailani's hands tremored, and she clenched them into fists. Daigo growled, and she looked up at him.

*Behind you.*

She turned her head and saw Lord Ishida and the others had gathered and were staring at her. Lord Ishida walked over to her.

"Is it true?" he asked lowly.

"Is what true, my Lord?"

"Are you a woman?"

Lailani frowned. What was he doing? He said he knew her secret and would never say anything, yet now he was questioning what he was already aware of. She looked past him at the sea of faces before her, their numbers half of what they were.

"You ..." she paused, not sure what to say.

"Let us speak privately," he said, motioning for her to follow him. He left the plaza and stood outside the torii. Lailani walked across the courtyard in silence, the eyes of her fellow soldiers watching curiously.

"Who are you?" he asked.

"My real name is Lailani."

"Whose dragon is that?"

"My father's."

Lord Ishida flicked his gaze at the creature, then back at her.

"He knows of your transgression?"

"Daigo or my father?"

"Your father."

"My father knows nothing," she said. "I left in the night. You act as though you are surprised, but you knew I was a woman."

Lord Ishida stiffened. "I did not."

"The night of the bonding ceremony, you told me you knew my secret. Did you forget?"

"That is not—" he stopped talking.

"I don't understand. If you didn't know I was a woman, then what secret did you mean?"

Realization dawned on her as soon as the words left her mouth. Her eyes widened, and she took a step back. He'd truly thought she was a man, which meant …

"It seems I was mistaken about you," he said harshly. "You know the law. No woman may bond with a dragon, nor serve in the emperor's army. How could you dishonor yourself in such a way?"

"I did it to protect my father," Lailani answered, choking back a sob.

"Then you dishonor your father as well. And his dragon."

"I didn't mean—"

"Silence!" Lord Ishida roared.

He lunged forward and grabbed her by the throat, squeezing painfully. She clawed at his hands, but his grip was like a vice. Fury burned in his eyes, and it frightened her. She heard Daigo roar, and a commotion broke out.

Lord Ishida jerked her around and pushed her back into the plaza. She fell face-first to the flagstones, scraping her palms and face. Lifting her head, she saw some of the other dragons had Daigo pinned down, his neck in one of their jaws.

"The punishment is death."

22

L AILANI WAITED FOR death to take her. A sword stabbed into a crack between the flagstones in front of her face.

"Rise," Lord Ishida demanded.

She pushed herself up onto her knees. The other soldiers stood quietly, watching. Lord Ishida stepped in front of her and pointed.

"We have all been deceived. This man is not a man at all, but a woman. The law says no woman may serve the empire, nor can one bond with a dragon. This dragon is not hers, but stolen from her father. She has committed many crimes in secret, but eventually, all things come into the light."

Lailani looked at Kalea. He was scowling at her. How would he feel once he learned exactly who she was?

"The punishment for her crimes is death. As an enforcer of the empire's laws, it is my duty to execute justice."

Lord Ishida pulled his sword from the ground and placed the tip against her neck. None of the soldiers voiced their opposition or made any move to stop him. They didn't owe her anything, but it still stung her to know that no one would speak up on her behalf. Huou would have. At least, that's what she believed. Daigo struggled, but he could not get free.

"I pronounce your guilt publicly, Lailani. Everyone here is a witness."

She saw Kalea's expression change. He knew who she was and opened his mouth to say something, then promptly closed it. Lord Ishida drew his blade back for a killing blow. Lailani bowed her head, too afraid to see it coming. A metal clang startled her, and she looked up. Lord Ishida's sword was on the flagstones.

"A life debt must be repaid," he said. "You saved Mahiro, and so I spare you. You are hereby banished from my company."

"Thank you for showing me mercy, my Lord."

"Did the dragon knowingly aid you?"

Lailani looked at Daigo. She could lie and save his life. No one would ever know.

*Tell him the truth.*

*But they will kill you.*

*I chose my path willingly, knowing the cost. You made an oath with me, and I kept my end. Now it is your turn to keep yours.*

Lailani nodded, tears spilling down her cheeks.

"The dragon will be executed for his crime."

Lord Ishida picked up his sword and strode to where Daigo was restrained.

*Please, little one. Honor your vow.*

"Wait!" Lailani cried out. "Let me do it!"

The commander turned and regarded her curiously.

"Please," she begged. "It is a matter of honor."

The words reminded her of the last conversation with her father. Hadn't he said the same thing? She didn't understand then what he'd meant and why he'd been so adamant about it, but she did now.

"What do you know of honor?" he asked.

"Let me do it."

Lord Ishida glanced at Shimura. They seemed to share an unspoken conversation, and Lord Ishida nodded.

"Very well. Come."

Lailani got to her feet and walked over to Daigo, accepting Lord Ishida's sword. The other dragons didn't move, but continued to keep him pinned down.

"Release him," she said. "He will not try to flee."

"How do I know this isn't a trick?"

"You don't. You'll just have to trust me."

Lord Ishida's face was hard to read. After a lengthy pause, he nodded. "Release him."

The dragons drew back and Daigo relaxed, lying down and curling his body around her. He turned his head to Lailani and met her gaze.

*I don't know if I can do this,* she said.

*You must. If I flee, they will hunt me down. And if you do not strike the blow, Lord Ishida will.*

*I'm so sorry, Daigo. I never meant for any of this to happen. I just wanted to protect father.*

*I know, little one, but plans often fail in flight. You can either tumble and learn or give up. You are stubborn like your father, so I know you will keep going. The amount of courage and strength you needed to come this far is more than most men have in them. Be proud.*

*I am afraid.*

*We all are at one time or another, but the feeling will pass. Press the tip of your sword here.*

Daigo used his talons to lift the scales on his chest. The flesh under the scales was also blue, though a much lighter hue. Lailani didn't move, so he used his tail to push her closer. She lifted the sword hesitantly, her hand trembling uncontrollably.

*I can't,* she said, breaking into a fit of crying.

*You must.*

She pressed the blade against his skin, but she had no intention of killing him. She had made the vow without knowing it would truly come to this. That had to negate the agreement somehow, didn't it?

Daigo closed his eyes and exhaled, his breath whipping her short hair about. *I am ready.*

The face of the man she killed in the pagoda flashed before her eyes. She couldn't do that to another living being again. How could anyone kill another person and not feel as if they themselves had died? She couldn't be the only one to feel that way.

*Daigo ...*

*Goodbye, Lailani.*

Daigo pushed her with his tail again, driving the blade into his flesh. His body jerked, and he grunted. Lailani clapped a hand over her mouth and screamed. Daigo shuddered as his blood poured from the wound, staining the sand and soaking into the ground. It only took a moment before he breathed his final breath and went still.

Lailani wrenched the sword free and threw it, turning to see Lord Ishida and the others watching her. The commander nodded once, his face solemn, and retrieved his thrown sword. Without another word, he climbed onto his dragon and departed the plaza. The others followed after him, either mounting their dragons or leaving through the torii to where their dragons waited.

Kalea was the last to go. He didn't look at her, instead stared at the ground. His presence offered some solace to her, but eventually, he sighed and left, and she was alone. No dragon companion, no friends, nothing but dead bodies to keep her company. She cried until there were no more tears.

Lord Ishida had left the dead behind with no burial or even a prayer to their ancestors. Lailani thought of Huou and entered the pagoda, her mind numb to the carnage around her. She grabbed Huou's legs and pulled him out of the building, his blood smearing the ground the entire way. He deserved to be buried, and she spent the next hour digging a hole in the sand beside Daigo until it was deep and long enough to fit him. Her hands ached by the time she finished, but it was a small cost to give him rest.

She wanted to bury the others, but she didn't have the heart or the strength for it. Instead, she knelt beside each person and prayed that their ancestors would welcome them. It was something, at least. Lailani went inside the pagoda to find her father's sword. It was near the back of the room, and she collected it and sheathed it at her waist.

The Roaran leader's body lay in the center of the blood-soaked floor. She didn't know who killed him. Everything had been so chaotic. His eyes were open, staring into nothingness as Huou's had been. A sense of compassion, though fleeting, washed over her. She walked to his body and ran her fingers over his eyelids, closing them. It was his fault that her secret was out, but there was no anger in her. There was only sadness.

Something caught her eye, something tucked into the armor on his chest. She grabbed it and went to the plaza. It was a parchment, folded in half. She opened it and read the script, not understanding what she was reading at first. Her eyes scanned the words again, and a third time.

Something didn't make sense. The letter mentioned a force in the east, but these Roarans had come through the pass on the west side. Their numbers were less than the letter said as well. The words at the bottom portion were covered with blood and hard to decipher. She gingerly wiped the fluid away and realization struck her.

This group of Roarans was a diversion, designed to throw them off. The force in the east was meant to converge on the emperor's army unsuspected. Lailani shoved the parchment into her armor and ran from the plaza, leaving the monastery behind. She needed to reach the front lines, needed to warn Kalea of the deception. She couldn't lose anyone else. The Shingtai Pass would be the quickest route, but she was on foot.

Lailani prayed she would get there before it was too late.

S HE FELT AMERATUS'S presence in her mind long before she saw the dragon. Lailani tried to ignore the creature, but she was still overcome with grief and the effort was too much. A shadow fell over her, and Ameratsu landed on the ground directly in front of her, blocking the way ahead.

She was blue like Daigo, but her scales were more vibrant. Ameratsu was a young dragon, that much was obvious by her smaller stature. She leaned in close to her.

*Why do you ignore me?*

*Leave me alone.*

She felt the dragon probing around in her mind, going through her memories. Lailani tried to force her out, but Ameratsu was the stronger of the two and the dragon pushed her feeble wall aside. It was similar to what the Roaran leader had done to her, but with Ameratsu, there was no pain.

*I am sorry that you lost your friends,* she said. *The pain you bear is heavy.*

*What do you want from me?* Lailani asked.

*You are a feisty one, though I sensed that before we bonded. Humans have an odd sense of loyalty that often overpowers their better judgment. I know that is why you pretended to be bonded to your father's dragon. What was his name?* Ameratsu probed further. *Ah, Daigo. A strong name.*

*Get out of my memories!*

*Calm yourself,* the dragon reprimanded gently. *I am trying to get to know you.*

*Why?*

*We are bound to each other.*

*I didn't ask to bond with you,* Lailani said.

*Not verbally, but I could sense it inside you. You've always wanted to be a rider. Now you are one, a true rider, and you are trying to push me away. You humans are confusing creatures.*

*Can you move out of the way? I have to get to my friend.*

Ameratsu probed her memories again.

*Kalea, yes? You have many memories of him. He must be a good friend.*

*He is. Now, move. He's walking into a trap, and if I don't warn him, he will die, too.*

*Where are you going?*

*To the border of Terran.*

*That's a long distance to travel by foot. It will take you many days.*

Days? Lailani's hopes shattered. Kalea would be dead by then. She felt the grief and anxiety rising within her again.

*I'm sorry,* the dragon said. *I did not mean to upset you. I can take you there if you let me. Flying is much faster than walking, but you know that.*

Lailani looked Ameratsu in the eyes. She saw herself reflected in the dragon's shiny gaze. She was covered in grime and dry blood and her expression was so serious, a far cry from the carefree girl she had been on the island not long ago. How had it only been a week since she left home? It felt like an eternity.

She considered the dragon's offer. Flying would get her there faster, but did she trust Ameratsu? The dragon had not given her any reason not to, but Lailani's fear of the unknown whispered doubts in the back of her mind. She reminded herself there were many lives at stake, not just Kalea's. If the imperial army was crushed by the Roarans, then there was nothing to stop them from rampaging across the country. If they reached the coast …

*Take me to the border,* Lailani said.

Ameratsu leaned in closer and tilted her head.

*Please.*

*That's better,* the dragon said. *You are not my master to issue such commands. It would be wise to remember that.*

*You are right. I'm sorry. You have shown me kindness, and I have been nothing but rude to you. Forgive me.*

*I forgive you,* Ameratsu said. *Now climb on and let's get you to your friends.*

*We could go back and get the saddle from Daigo's body.*

The dragon snorted. *No saddle for me. I can't stand the things. Come on.*

Ameratsu's personality differed vastly from Daigo's, and Lailani knew it was going to take some time getting used to the dragon. She climbed up the dragon's shoulder and onto her back, finding hand and footholds between Ameratsu's scales. Once she was settled, the dragon launched into the air.

The ride was rough, but Lailani didn't complain. She couldn't believe a dragon not only had bonded with her, but that one *wanted* to. Despite the fact that Daigo had helped her, she doubted he would have bonded with her had he not been tied to her father.

*Why did you bond with me? It's unlawful for a woman to be a rider, let alone a soldier. You risk being executed like ... like Daigo was.*

*I thought you deserved the opportunity.*

*You know nothing about me.*

*Not yet, but time will change that.*

*If we survive this.*

They flew through the Shingtai Pass and out of the Shojin Mountains. Ameratsu turned northeast at the base of the crags and they sped over the landscape. It wasn't long before the first sign of battle became visible. Smoke billowed up from the ground, filling the sky, and Lailani's heart raced as Ameratsu flew into the dark clouds.

She lost sight of everything for a brief moment, and then they broke through the other side of the smoke. Devastation was everywhere. Bodies littered the ground, both friend and foe, and she even saw the corpses of dragons. Shouts of alarm reached her ears, but she was focused on the imperial defenses.

They were abandoned.

Lailani scanned the area, but there were no signs of the imperial army. The Roarans had overrun the defenses with siege towers and weapons of war. A barrage of arrows flew up at them from the ground, but they bounced harmlessly off Ameratsu's scales. The dragon weaved through the air, evading more of the projectiles.

Something massive came hurtling at them. Before Ameratsu could dodge it, an explosion ripped through the air beside them. Lailani's ears rang, and she was blinded. The dragon must have been, too, because she slammed into the side of a siege tower, toppling the structure in a shower of splinters and screaming men. Lailani held on as tightly as she could, but the force of the collision sent her crashing to the ground.

Dazed, she struggled to her feet and looked around. Roarans were closing in from every side, and Ameratsu wasn't moving. Was she dead?

*Ameratsu?*

*That's going to hurt for a few days,* the dragon huffed.

*We need to get out of here!*

Panic flooded the bond, overwhelming Lailani's senses.

*I can't move,* Ameratsu said. *Something is holding me down.*

Lailani staggered over to the debris, but she couldn't see anything pinning the dragon in place.

*I don't see anything.*

She feared Ameratsu might have broken something and was paralyzed. The Roaran soldiers flooded around her, and Lailani drew her sword. She swung the blade, cleaving limbs and adding to the pile of bodies surrounding her. With her small amount of training, she laid waste to anyone who got near her. It became clear that these men weren't warriors. They were fodder.

Death followed every swing of her sword. Some of the Roarans fell back, stumbling over the bodies of the fallen, but those who were foolish enough to think they could oppose her fell to the rise and fall of her blade.

More Roarans joined the mob around her, and through the haze of bloodlust, she saw a man with no armor push through the crowd. Why would he come unarmed and unprotected? She realized the truth too late. A glowing orb formed in his hand and he hurled it at her. Lailani turned and ran, but the magic struck her in the back. Searing heat and pain erupted along her entire body. Her armor did nothing to diminish the power of the spell.

Lailani collapsed near Ameratsu, her body heavy like stone. She couldn't even lift her head, and she watched helplessly as the soldiers closed in. One of them kicked her in the face. The world blurred. Her mind was cloudy, her thoughts sluggish. Time seemed to still, and then darkness seeped in from all sides.

WHEN LAILANI OPENED her eyes, she found herself in a dimly lit tent. She was sitting upright in a chair, her wrists and ankles bound to it with rope. She was alone, but the loud voices of many men reached her from the outside.

*You're awake,* Ameratsu said. *Are you all right?*

*I think so. Where am I? Where are you?*

*They carried you away, but I didn't see where they took you. I'm still stuck where I landed. It seems there are a few sorcerers keeping me from moving. Maybe if you kill some of them, I'll be able to free myself.*

*We're both prisoners. Assuming I can escape, how would I kill a couple of sorcerers on my own without being captured again?*

*With magic,* Ameratsu said simply.

*I'm not a sorcerer.*

*Maybe not, but riders often gain magical abilities from their dragons. Perhaps you have.*

*How would I know?*

*I'm not sure. I'm not a human.*

Lailani rolled her eyes. Ameratsu wasn't very helpful. She struggled against her bonds, but they were so tight her fingers were turning blue. A glance around the tent didn't reveal much. The furnishings were limited, and she didn't see her sword. Daylight filled the tent abruptly as someone entered behind her. She heard them rustling around but dared not look back. After a moment, a man stepped into her view. He looked at her and smiled.

"Welcome back."

His voice held an accent she'd never heard before, but his armor was the same as the Roarans from the monastery: overlapping plates of metal on the arms and legs and a flared helmet. A curved blade was sheathed at his waist, and he rested his hand on the hilt.

"What is your name?"

"Why should I tell you?"

"You can be difficult if you want. It makes no difference to me. I'm not a barbarian, as you might believe. I'm just trying to have a civil discourse with you."

"Invading another country and slaughtering its people is barbaric to me."

"For those with simple minds, perhaps it is. But I am not a simple man. The empire is crumbling. It was even before our armies marched upon it. As a lowly peasant, there is much you are not privy to. Entertain me for a moment and imagine an enemy who poses as an ally. How would you know whether their words are true, or a deceit meant to take your power?"

Lailani didn't know what he was talking about. She remained silent.

"The emperor is a snake, one that seeks to consume his own children. Our people are one, but the imperial family has divided us. I will not dull you with a history lesson, but understand that we do not invade a foreign country out of boredom. We come to take our homeland back. If that means blood must be spilled, then so be it."

"What of the innocent? Those who do not care about who rules over them? They suffer unnecessarily."

"There is always collateral damage in war, but we would never harm the innocent intentionally. Once the emperor is dead and we have secured the throne, we will help those who were harmed."

"You can't bring back the dead," Lailani said, thinking of Huou.

"No, we cannot."

"Why am I here?"

"Why indeed? The imperial army pulled back to the palace. So why would a lone dragon rider be flying overhead? You are obviously a spy."

"I'm no spy," she said. "I'm not even part of the imperial army."

"You wear the armor and you ride a dragon. It doesn't take much perception to see that."

"I was part of the army, but I've been banished. I just want to go home."

"Do you live on this battlefield? I do not think so. You are here for a reason. Why?"

Lailani didn't owe the man any explanations, but she didn't see any reason to lie, either.

"I was coming to warn my friend."

"About what?"

"About your force in the east. I didn't want to lose another person who is dear to me. When I arrived and saw the army was gone, I didn't know what to think. Your men attacked me and my dragon without provocation."

"The emperor recalled his men to the palace when he saw our war machines. He hides like a coward behind his walls, but they will fall just like his empire. As for you, the sight of your dragon was provocation enough. Do you know how many Roarans have been terrorized by the emperor's dragon riders? I'm sure you don't."

"Will you let me go?" Lailani asked.

"Why should I?"

"I have done nothing to you. I want to return to my home."

The man stepped closer to her and leaned down, his lips inches from her ear.

"How did a woman become a soldier without being caught? Or is that why they banished you?"

His breath tingled her skin and she fought the natural urge to shudder. How did he know she was a woman?

"I had help."

"Your dragon?"

"No. My father's."

"So you are not bonded to the beast?"

"I am bonded to the dragon I came here with. The dragon who helped me pass as a man was my father's dragon. He's dead now."

The man stood straight, and she was glad he was no longer near her face.

"You have seen the cruelty of the emperor's ways. In the new empire, there will be no such rules against women. I have women among my ranks. They serve as soldiers, sorcerers, and many other positions of power. Why do you think the emperor forbids women from serving the empire?"

Lailani had heard many stories over the years. Some believed it was because blood begets blood and since women shed blood, to let them wield a blade would mean more blood would be spilled. That one didn't make any sense to her. Another theory was that it had something to do with the emperor's daughter.

"I don't know," she answered.

"It is because he fears women. Many claim that men are the strongest, and that may be true physically, but women are tenacious beings. Their fortitude is unimaginable. You are an example of that. Posing as a man, fighting for your place among them. Surely it hasn't been easy."

The man was right. If women were allowed to serve, how many sonless fathers would have been saved? More than she could count. Still, the way the Roarans were going about orchestrating their change was wrong.

"I have a proposition for you," he said.

His eyes traversed her body, lingering longer at her lap than anywhere else. She feared he was going to say something crude.

"I want you and your dragon to join us."

Lailani's face scrunched, not expecting those words.

"No."

"You didn't give it much thought, did you? I don't blame you. It will take time for you to forget the years of indoctrination you've endured. I offer you two paths. The other is death."

His expression darkened.

"I would hate to kill you and your dragon, but I will do it."

Lailani believed him. She didn't want to die, but she refused to betray her people. Lord Ishida had banished her, true, but that didn't mean she didn't care for his safety. She was just as confused and hurt as he was. They had shared a moment, one that she would always treasure, and learning that he wasn't after a woman's heart would not change that.

"I will give you some time to consider my offer. When I return, I hope you will make the right decision."

He started to leave, and Lailani called out, "Wait. You asked for my name. It's Lailani."

"Lailani. It's beautiful and strong. Like you. My name is Tchi."

He left the tent, and she was alone again. She would never join the Roarans, but if she refused, she and Ameratsu would be executed.

*The Roarans want us to ally with them,* Lailani told the dragon.

*Fools. I'll flame their entire camp once I can move again.*

*If we don't join them, they'll kill us.*

*I don't like those options.*

*Neither do I, but what can we do?*

*Make our own option. Escape.*

*Any ideas on how?*

*Not yet.*

Lailani tried to get her hands free of the ropes again, but the chord bit into her flesh. She hissed in pain and gave up. There had to be some way out of this predicament.

*Wait, I have an idea,* she said. *We'll use the Roarans' own tricks against them.*

*What tricks?*

*Deception. The force they sent through the Shingtai Pass was a diversion, and they fooled us into thinking the bodies on the floor were all dead.*

Lailani projected the memory to Ameratsu through the bond, one of the many lessons Master Satoshi had taught them.

*Clever. How will you convince him that we've switched sides?*

*The one I spoke to, Tchi, knows I was banished. I can tell him that we'll agree to help in exchange for the safety of my friends and family. In his mind, my loyalty to the emperor is from indoctrination.*

*You think he will believe that?*

*I have to make him.*

*It's our best option,* Ameratsu said.

*It's our* only *option.*

*True.*

*I'll try to gain his trust. Once we get close to the palace, the charade ends. You need to be just as convincing. If the sorcerers release you and you try to fly off, I don't think you'll get very far.*

*I wouldn't leave you behind to save my own scales.*

*That's good to know. I appreciate it.*

They had a plan. Now all she had to do was swallow her revulsion and play the part of a stage performer.

25

L AILANI WAS DOZING off when Tchi returned. The temperature within the tent was warm, stuffy even, and it made her sleepy. She stretched as much as she could to wake herself, and the Roaran leader strode past her and grabbed something off of a small desk.

"Have you made a decision?" he asked, glancing at her.

"Yes. I will help you."

A grin spread across his lips. "Good. I'm glad you were swayed by reason. I assume your dragon is of the same mind as you?"

"She is."

"That is most excellent news. We're marching to the palace at sundown. Your dragon can see in the dark, yes?"

*He doesn't know much about dragons,* Lailani told Ameratsu.

*That's not surprising. He's a Roaran, not a Terran.*

"Yes, she can see great in the dark."

Tchi nodded, seeming pleased. "You will, of course, have to prove that your loyalty no longer resides with the emperor before I trust you to roam the camp freely."

"Ask and it shall be done." She hoped she wasn't overselling herself.

"Eager, are you? That is good."

He walked over to her and drew a dagger from his waist and cut the ropes that bound her hands and feet. Lailani lifted her arms and gingerly rubbed her wrists. The skin was sensitive and red.

"Come with me."

Tchi left the tent. Lailani followed after him, wondering what he had planned. The camp was swarming with hundreds of soldiers, if not thousands. They were going in every direction, and it was clear they were preparing to march on the palace. Tchi led her to a section of the camp where long posts had been erected. A dozen or more prisoners were all spread out, chained to iron rings that were attached to the posts. They were imperial soldiers.

"These men were caught trying to sabotage our supply train. Imperial scum doing the bidding of their emperor."

Lailani looked at each one briefly. They wore hardened expressions. Grime and blood covered most of them, but nobody appeared to be injured.

"Do you plan to release them once you kill the emperor?" she asked.

"You have a lot to learn about war," Tchi replied. He pointed to a man at the far end of the posts. "I want you to kill that one."

Lailani did her best not to wear her emotions on her face, but inside, she was panicking.

"I said I wanted you to prove yourself to me. This is how you will do so."

"As you command," Lailani said. It surprised her that her voice didn't crack with the words. "Will it be with my sword or one of yours?"

"His death will come from Roaran steel."

Tchi drew the curved sword from the scabbard that hung from his belt and handed it to her hilt first. She took the sword and frantically tried to figure out how she was going to get out of the situation alive. If she killed Tchi, she wouldn't get far. And she couldn't kill an imperial soldier. Even if what Tchi had said was true about the Roaran's reason for invading, the Terran soldier was doing his duty. There was no crime in that.

*The wide world is a place full of cruelty and power-hungry people.*

Daigo's words echoed in her mind. She didn't believe him when he'd said that to her. Yet now … now it was all she saw.

*He wants me to kill an imperial soldier.*

*Let me see through your eyes.*

Lailani's eyelids twitched, and she blinked a few times. She didn't notice anything different, but Ameratsu's presence filled her mind in a way she hadn't experienced before. It felt intrusive.

*Fourteen prisoners,* the dragon said. *And he only wants you to kill one?*

*Yes.*

*Do it.*

Lailani's face scrunched in shock. *What?*

*You must convince him he has your loyalty. If one man must die to save thousands more, it is not so great a cost.*

*You don't truly believe that,* Lailani said.

*I do.*

"If you can't do it, then I can't trust you. And if there is no trust between us, then I must kill you."

*It's my life or his? That hardly seems fair. It is not my place to decide who lives or dies.*

*Today it is,* Ameratsu replied. *They are going to die regardless, whether by your hand or that of a Roaran. At least you can make it quick and painless. The Roarans will probably torture him first. Death at your hands may be a blessing.*

The face of the man she'd killed at the monastery flooded her mind. The sheer terror in his eyes was enough to make her wish she'd never picked up a sword.

"Time is running out," Tchi said, his tone turning impatient.

"Forgive me. I was speaking with my dragon."

Lailani walked over to the man Tchi had indicated and looked down at him. His dark eyes met hers, and there was no fear in them. She knelt and lowered her voice.

"You know what is coming." It was a statement as much as a question.

His gaze flicked to Tchi and back to her. He nodded slightly.

"I will make it quick."

She rose and placed the tip of the blade against his windpipe, then looked over her shoulder at Tchi. The look on his face was like that of a predator intent upon its prey. He was enjoying this. She turned her attention back to the imperial soldier and licked her lips. She hadn't been able to kill Daigo, and she doubted she had the fortitude to kill this man.

"I die for the emperor," the soldier whispered. "Send me to my rest."

Lailani slid the blade forward, cutting into the man's throat and ending his life. He made a wet choking sound and fell over, the sword making the wound bigger as he went down. She clenched her jaw and swallowed hard, forcing the bile back down. It was as if she was in a nightmare, only she knew she wasn't asleep. She wiped the blade on the soldier's clothes and turned to face Tchi.

"Do you trust me now?"

Tchi smiled. He did that a lot, and she hated him for it.

"Anyone can kill a single man when it's necessary," he said. "But few can kill fourteen. Kill the rest of them."

The words crashed around her like dark ocean waves. He'd lied to her, but of course he had. He was a Roaran. Her blood boiled, consuming her guilt and fear, burning it in the flames of her rage. She envisioned running at him, swinging the sword and removing his head from his shoulders. It was tempting.

*He wants me to kill them all.*

*I know. I'm still watching.*

*I can't,* Lailani said.

*You* can. *You don't want to.*

*Why would I? It's an act of evil!*

Ameratsu didn't disagree with her, but she remained silent. The dragon flooded their bond with sympathy. The truth hit her, heavy as a blow. She had to do it. There was no other way to convince him of her loyalty otherwise. Her stomach churned with repulsion and anxiety. Tchi stared at her, his eyes searching hers for a sign of weakness. He wouldn't find any, because she hid it behind a wall of rage.

Lailani looked at the next soldier. He stared straight ahead, ignoring both of her and Tchi. She strode over to him and swung the sword quickly, slicing his throat. Blood poured from the wound, coating his armor and running onto the ground. Lailani didn't stop there. She went to the third man and killed him, too. And the fourth. And the fifth.

She strode from one to the next, snuffing their lives out without mercy. In the back of her mind, she knew she would never recover from this moment. She knew, too, that it was a matter of necessity. It was her or them, and she wasn't ready to die. Ameratsu's presence fled from her mind after the first few kills. Lailani didn't blame the dragon. She didn't want to see it either, but now it was burned into her memory like a fiery brand on flesh.

She slaughtered them. All fourteen. When the last soldier was dead, she wiped the blade off and offered it back to Tchi. She was dead inside, and her face was devoid of any emotion.

"Impressive," Tchi said, eyeing her warily. "You have no mercy for your enemies. I see a bright future for you among us. You've earned my trust. If there is anything you need, say it. Nothing will be denied to you."

"Thank you … my Lord." The words were hollow, meaningless.

"You are free to roam the camp."

Lailani left him and went to where Ameratsu was being held. The dragon couldn't move, but her eyes settled on Lailani.

*You are stronger than steel.*

Lailani didn't say anything. She sat down in the debris beside the dragon and stared off blankly in the palace's direction. Night couldn't come soon enough.

W HEN DUSK CAME, the sorcerers released Ameratsu from their magic. The dragon rose to her feet slowly, stretching her sinuous body. The soldiers who'd been standing guard nearby slowly backed away and left them alone.

*What's our plan?*

*As soon as we get close to the palace, we break away from the Roarans and get inside,* Lailani said.

*And then what?*

Lailani had been wondering that herself. She kept her mind busy to keep from being overwhelmed by the emotions that threatened to consume her. Fourteen of her countrymen were dead at her hands. She shook the thoughts away.

*I need to find Kalea and warn him about the danger. Tchi said the emperor pulled his forces back to the palace because of the war machines. They still don't know about the force coming from the east.*

*The emperor will be caught between two blades,* Ameratsu mused. *You should warn your friend, but you also need to tell the emperor what's coming. The dragon riders may yet be able to get him to safety.*

Lailani was so worried about Kalea that she hadn't even considered that. She had thought herself ready to play at war, but there was so much she wasn't prepared for.

*Yes, I will find a way to warn the emperor. Perhaps Lord Ishida will listen before calling the guards on me.*

*Your feelings toward him are strong. Do you love him?*

Lailani laughed bitterly. *I don't love him. I liked him, but that doesn't matter. Nothing will happen between us.*

*Because of your deception?*

*Because I'm a woman. He prefers the company of men.*

Ameratsu pushed her head against Lailani, nuzzling her as an oversized horse would.

*You're no longer alone,* the dragon said. *You have my companionship now.*

Lailani ran her hands along Ameratsu's smooth scales. It was still difficult for her to believe that a dragon had chosen her, a woman. Her lifelong dream was now a reality. She didn't know what the future held for them after this was all over, but they would face the adversity together.

*Why did you ignore me? When we first bonded, you shut me out.*

*I was afraid our bonding was going to disrupt my plans. I convinced Daigo to come with me to protect my father. Bonding with another dragon felt like I was betraying him, even though he wasn't mine.*

*You humans overthink too much.*

*Dragons don't?*

*Of course not. We're the wisest beings in existence.*

Pride filled the bond, and Lailani smiled. It was still possible to experience joy, even though she had been through a nightmare. The sound of many feet approaching turned Lailani's attention to Tchi. Six heavily armed guards were with him.

"Are you ready for our assault on the palace?"

Lailani stood up, brushing splinters and dust from her armor.

"We are ready, my Lord."

"Excellent. I've sent scouts ahead to ensure no traps are awaiting us. You and your dragon will take the lead. If riders come out to stop us, my sorcerers will deal with them. Your only focus is to open the main gates to give us entry."

"What if something happens to us?"

"Your loss would be regrettable, but we have other ways inside. I have men waiting in the sewers, but that's not an effective entrance. The tunnels are too narrow to allow enough men through to overwhelm their defenses."

"What about the force in the east?" Lailani asked.

"They are waiting for my signal."

"They won't attack me by accident, will they?"

"I can't guarantee anything, but they should be focused on their own task."

Lailani wanted to ask what their task was, but she didn't want to press too much and draw his distrust. She nodded.

"Can I have my sword back?"

"I can give you a better one," Tchi said, reaching for his own blade.

"No." She saw his frown and hurriedly said, "It's my father's. I want to bring him honor tonight."

Tchi leaned over to one of his guards and whispered something. The man bowed and sprinted away, returning a moment later carrying her father's weapon. He handed it to Tchi, who in turn offered it to Lailani.

"May your blade swing true."

Lailani accepted the sword and strapped the scabbard chord around her waist. So far, everything was going as she expected.

"Make sure to keep yourself at the front of the army," Tchi said. "If you get too far ahead, my sorcerers will not be able to protect you from the other riders."

"I will make sure she flies slow."

Tchi looked from Lailani to Ameratsu. He stared at the dragon intently for a moment, then looked toward the palace. Lailani followed his gaze and spotted a flash of light in the sky.

"That is the sign that all is clear," he said. "Let us go and bring down an empire."

Tchi left with his guards, and Lailani climbed onto Ameratsu's back.

*I don't like him,* the dragon said. *His soul is dark.*

*He's wicked,* Lailani agreed. *I pray to my ancestors that he falls quickly in this battle.*

Ameratsu flexed her muscles and leaped into the air, slowly spiraling higher above the camp. From her vantage point, Lailani could see a dark mass at the front of the camp, creeping along the road leading to the palace.

*There are so many of them.*

Unless they experienced a miracle, she did not doubt that the empire would indeed crumble this night. She tried to keep the faint flicker of hope alive by telling herself that if the emperor got to safety, they could regroup somehow and drive the Roarans away.

Ameratsu flew above the mass of soldiers, her pace slow and subdued. The calm atmosphere betrayed the racing of Lailani's heart. Chaos and death were only moments away.

*Please give us victory,* she silently prayed.

The army marched past the abandoned defenses, their shadowy bulk consuming the smaller shades of darkness that dotted the landscape. A multitude of torches illuminated the walls of the imperial city, but from this distance, Lailani couldn't see much else.

*Do you see any guards?*

*Yes,* Ameratsu answered. *The walls are crawling with them. Look.*

Lailani's vision blurred for a moment. When the distortion cleared, she was seeing things through the dragon's eyes. A wide moat full of water surrounded the front half of the city. The bridge that spanned it was drawn up, keeping the fortress sealed from outsiders. *Except for the sewers,* she reminded herself. A rectangular plaza lay beyond the first wall, and a second, thicker wall protected the inner city. A third wall wrapped around the palace, the multi-tiered pagoda rising from the center of the city like a snake poised to strike.

Atop the walls, imperial soldiers milled about, oblivious to the approaching Roarans. Oddly, there was no sign of any dragons. Was it possible they had already evacuated the emperor from the palace?

*The riders are here,* Ameratsu said. *I cannot see them, but I can sense their presence. They are hiding.*

*In fear?*

*Dragons fear nothing.*

*I've seen enough.*

Lailani took one last look around the city before her vision returned to normal. She tightened her grip on Ameratsu's scales when the wind picked up, the gusts buffeting her roughly. A saddle would have made her feel safer, but there was nothing to be done about that now.

The Roaran army swarmed up the road slowly, their dark mass devouring everything. Ameratsu kept pace with them, her long blue body undulating lazily through the sky.

*We're inching closer,* the dragon said.

Lailani could see the walls more clearly now, but they were still too far away to make a run for it. Time passed slowly as the army encroached closer and closer. Once they were a few hundred feet away, Lailani found it odd that none of the guards on the wall had sounded an alarm.

*How do they not see the Roarans?*

Before Ameratsu could offer an answer, an explosion rocked the ground below. Lailani peered down around the dragon's neck and saw a flaming ball bouncing down the road toward the Roaran army. As it crashed among their ranks, the ball erupted, sending flames in every direction and lighting soldiers on fire. A chorus of bells began ringing from the watchtowers that ringed the city.

*It seems their presence has been discovered,* Ameratsu said gleefully.

Lailani eyed the distance between them and the wall. With the confusion below, Tchi's sorcerers likely wouldn't be able to stop them.

*Let's go!*

Ameratsu shot forward, speeding through the sky. The wall grew bigger as they closed in, and with it, Lailani's hope grew as well. Suddenly, Ameratsu jerked to a halt. Lailani flung forward, smacking her head into the dragon's neck.

*What are you doing?* She cried out.

*Something is keeping me from going any further.*

*The emperor's defenses?*

*No.* Ameratsu swiveled her head back to look at the Roarans. *It's them.*

Apparently, Tchi's trust only went so far. Lailani ground her teeth in frustration.

*He said he wanted us to open the gates. We can't do that if he's keeping a tight leash.*

*Unless he doesn't truly need us to open them.*

The men in the sewers. They were the ones who would open the gates. Lailani shook her head. Another ruse. She'd thought she was a step ahead of Tchi, but it turned out to be a step behind. She eyed the distance, a foolish idea coming to her.

*Retreat over the army and try again.*

*Why? Their magic is too strong.*

*I'm going to fly on my own.*

AMERATSU DID AS she asked and flew further away from the wall. Lailani projected what she envisioned through the bond. At first, Ameratsu protested, but Lailani was adamant. It was a dangerous risk, but it was the only idea she could come up with.

*Are you sure about this?*

*No, but let's not question that.*

*Very well.*

Lailani got into a crouch and dug her fingers deep under Ameratsu's neck scales. The dragon launched ahead. The wind whipped at Lailani's face, stinging her eyes. She prepared herself for the abrupt stop she knew was coming.

When Ameratsu's bulk jolted, Lailani released her grip. She went flying over the dragon's head. Her stomach dropped, and a scream tore free of her throat. Gravity immediately pulled her toward the ground, and she descended faster than she expected. She would not make it over the wall.

Lailani stretched her arms out and forced her eyes to stay open. She slammed into the wall, her hands scrambling for purchase on the smooth stones. The skin rubbed from her fingertips, sending flaring pain through her hands. Her feet slid on the front of the wall, and she was about to fall when a soldier's face appeared over the ledge.

"Help me," she huffed. "I have a message for Lord Ishida."

The man grabbed hold of her wrists and pulled her up. She knelt, glad to have something solid under her.

"Who are you? How did you get up here?"

Lailani pointed over the wall. "My dragon is back there. The Roarans have captured her. I need to speak to Lord Ishida."

The soldier had a confused look on his face, looking from her to the army of Roarans beyond the wall.

"There's another force coming from the east," she said. "You need to inform the emperor. Hurry!"

Her shout snapped him out of his confusion. He ran to the nearby watchtower, but she didn't wait to see what he was doing. She ran along the wall and down the stairs into the plaza. The gate of the second wall leading into the city was still open, and as she ran toward it, she saw why. Imperial soldiers were pulling back from the first wall. They were giving up ground already?

Explosions erupted over the city, lighting up the night sky. Something heavy cracked against the wall behind her, sending tremors through the ground. Tchi's war machines.

*Are you all right?*

*Yes. No one has noticed your departure. I'm surprised you made it.*

*So am I,* Lailani admitted. *I'll come back for you as soon as I'm done here.*

She joined a group of imperial soldiers rushing through the second gate. The city streets were empty, but a few children looked out the windows of their homes curiously before being reprimanded by their fearful parents.

Ameratsu said the dragon riders were hiding, but she saw nothing that could conceal their presence. The structures of the city were too small and spaced out. Her eyes went to the palace. They would probably be there, protecting the emperor. Lailani sprinted down the principal thoroughfare, her footsteps echoing off the surrounding buildings.

The gate leading to the palace was closed, and a contingent of imperial soldiers three men deep stood in front of it. Lailani slowed her pace and offered a hurried bow.

"I need to speak with Lord Ishida," she said breathlessly. "Is he with the emperor?"

An officer stepped forward, his hand on the hilt of his sword.

"No one is allowed into the palace. Why aren't you with the others on the wall?"

"I'm part of Lord Ishida's clan. He left me behind to scout the Shingtai Pass. I must speak with him. It's urgent." She doubted the man would know she was lying.

The officer stepped closer, his eyes scrutinizing her facial features.

"What is your name?"

"Lai Seijin," she answered. "Please, sir. Time is already running out."

The man turned around and whistled. A moment later, the thick wooden gates opened and the officer waved her through. She ran across the threshold and looked up at the towering pagodas that comprised the palace. Their stone bases were six feet in height, and carved into the front of them were long steps leading to the main doors. Dragons were stationed all around the palace, their riders mounted and ready for battle.

The gate slammed shut behind her, breaking her reverie. One of the riders dismounted and came striding toward her. A wave of relief washed over her when she saw it was Kalea.

"What are you doing here?" he asked, glancing at the other riders behind him.

"I could ask you the same thing. Why haven't you evacuated the emperor?"

"He refuses to leave."

"Why?"

"He doesn't believe the city can be conquered. Lord Ishida banished you. Why did you come here?"

"I came to warn you," she said. "The Roarans have another force coming from the east."

"How do you know?"

Lailani pulled out the folded parchment she'd found at the monastery and handed it to him. He opened it, his eyes skimming over the words. The color in his face drained.

"We're trapped," he muttered.

"You need to get everyone out of here, if that's even still a possibility. Where's Lord Ishida?"

"He's with the emperor."

"We need to warn him. Maybe together we can convince the emperor to flee somewhere. The school can keep him safe. Then we can rally our forces and drive the Roarans out."

"I admire the optimism, but ..." Kalea shook his head. "The emperor is stubborn and set in his ways. He will not change his mind. He claims help is coming."

"From where?"

"He won't say."

"We have to at least try to talk to him."

"Lailani ..." He sighed. "I'm sorry."

"For what?"

"I didn't speak up when Lord Ishida treated you the way he did at the monastery. We're friends. I should have said something, but I was afraid. And now your dragon is dead."

"I wish you would have, but I know all too well how fear can control you. Daigo wasn't bound to me. He was my father's dragon."

They stared at one another in silence for a moment, and then Lailani said, "I buried Huou."

Kalea nodded, his eyes glossing with tears. "I hated leaving our brothers like that, but Lord Ishida … I'm sorry. I wish I had half the strength you do."

Lailani was taken aback by his compliment. She smiled. "Come with me. We need to warn the emperor of what's coming. What he does with the knowledge is for him to decide."

"You risk death," Kalea said. "Women are not allowed before the emperor without his permission."

"He doesn't know I'm a woman."

"Lord Ishida does."

"I am not afraid. Not anymore."

She strode past him and walked up the stairs that led to the palace. Kalea remained behind. A pair of servants rushed to open the doors for her, and she entered the interior of the building. In the center of the room was a throne that sat upon a raised platform. Sitting in the chair was an aged man with short gray hair. He wore expensive robes that shimmered under the torchlight, and standing nearby was Lord Ishida.

Lailani steeled her emotions and walked toward the throne. A plush red rug lined the walkway leading to it, and she kept her eyes fixed ahead. Lord Ishida looked up as she approached and his surprise vanished as quickly as it appeared. His face flushed with his anger and he rested his hand on the hilt of his sword.

"Your Majesty," Lailani called out. "I come bearing news."

She stopped a few feet from the throne and knelt, bowing forward until her forehead touched the ground.

"Rise," the emperor said, his voice stronger than she expected. "What news do you have?"

Lailani stood, flicking her gaze to Lord Ishida briefly before focusing on the emperor.

"The Roarans have a second army. They are coming from the opposite direction with the intent of blocking us in. You need to flee the palace for your safety."

"Our enemy may surround us, but they are like wolves howling at the moon. The sound may frighten those weak of heart, but there is nothing to fear. They will not breach our walls."

Lailani knew she needed to tread carefully with her words if she wanted to leave the palace alive. Lord Ishida would probably enjoy executing her if the emperor ordered it.

"Your Majesty, have you seen their force? Their numbers are like the sand. I implore you to escape to safety. You are the hope of Terran. Wherever you go, your people will follow. We can regroup and gather our strength—"

"Why does a lowly soldier think to lecture me?" The emperor stood and glared at her. "I am the

Emperor of Terran, the Heavenly Sovereign. I hold the final word on all things and I will *not* leave this palace unless the gods say otherwise."

A sound like thunder rumbled, and the palace shuddered. Lord Ishida drew his sword, whirling around and looking up at the ceiling. The back wall of the palace bowed inward, creaking as it bent the laws of nature before exploding in a shower of debris. Lailani threw herself to the floor.

She rolled onto her side and watched in horror as the ceiling collapsed onto the throne.

THE EMPEROR WAS dead.

Lailani could tell by the way the old man's body lie mangled beneath the ceiling beams. She picked her way through the devastation, looking for Lord Ishida. He was crawling out from under a pile of debris.

"Are you all right?" she asked.

"I'm fine. Check on the emperor."

"He's dead."

Lord Ishida stood and looked at her. "Are you sure?"

She nodded. His expression turned grim.

"The empire has fallen."

"Not yet," Lailani said. "What of his heir?"

"His only son died last year from sickness. The empress followed soon after from a broken heart."

"Was the emperor an only child?"

Lord Ishida shook his head. "No, but none of his siblings are alive."

"Kalea told me the emperor said help was coming. Do you know what he meant?"

"No. He would divulge nothing to me. I suspect it was his pride speaking and there is no help truly coming."

Lord Ishida turned to look at the wall that was blown in. Through the hole, Lailani could see the rolling hills beyond the walls. The second force of Roarans had arrived, and they had brought war machines with them just as Tchi had. They were surrounded with no escape.

"You should have forced the emperor to leave," she said.

Lord Ishida turned back to face her. "I tried to convince him. He wouldn't go. It shouldn't matter to you, anyway. I banished you. Why did you come?"

"I was trying to warn you of what was coming. I was too late, but we can still fight."

"Fight for what? The emperor is dead. Without him, there is no empire."

"Do the innocent people of Terran mean nothing? *They* are the empire, not the emperor."

"Blasphemy."

"You know it's true. I heard you talking to Shimura about the emperor. The things you said could be considered blasphemy as well."

"You are a liar *and* a spy? Your treachery knows no bounds."

Lailani could only laugh in frustration.

"I know I deceived you, but I had no other choice. I could not allow my father to go to war. He would have died. I had hoped you would understand my reasons given what the emperor did to your father, but it seems I was mistaken."

She turned to leave and the doors burst open. Kalea and a handful of other guards were there. Lailani climbed over the debris and pushed past them.

"Don't bother," she said. "The emperor has fallen."

"What happened? Where are you going?" Kalea followed after her.

"Something struck the palace and part of the ceiling crushed the emperor. The enemy now has the imperial city surrounded, and Lord Ishida is more concerned with how I deceived him. If you want to stay here and serve him, do so, but I am going to fight to protect the people."

She did not know how she was going to free Ameratsu from the Roaran magic that bound her, but she couldn't leave the dragon out there alone. Lailani looked at Kalea.

"I must ask a favor of you."

"What is it?"

"Can you take me to my dragon?"

"I thought Daigo was dead?"

"I told you, Daigo wasn't mine. I bonded with *her*." Lailani pointed to the sky where Ameratsu was.

"A dragon bonded with a woman? Now I have seen everything."

"Never mind. I will go on my own."

"No!"

Kalea stepped forward and gently grabbed onto her arm.

"I'm sorry. I didn't mean to offend you. I'm surprised, is all. It is against the law, and I never thought I would see a dragon brave such a risk." He stared into her eyes with a solemn expression.

"I'm sorry," he said again. "I will take you."

Lailani walked with him to where his dragon waited. The creature swiveled his head to watch her as she climbed onto his back, and Kalea hurried over to each member of his command. He rejoined her and climbed into the saddle, seating himself in front of her. She wrapped her arms around him and held on tightly.

The dragon leaped into the air, and the other dragon riders followed behind them. They passed over the quiet city and both walls that protected it. The imperial soldiers defending the main gates were shooting arrows down at the Roarans. The enemy hadn't breached the gate yet, but they were slowly inching their battering rams closer.

"Tell your dragon to be careful!" she shouted above the wind. "Tchi has sorcerers that can immobilize him!"

Kalea nodded. They flew over the Roaran army and as Kalea's dragon drew close to Ameratsu, Lailani prepared herself to jump onto the dragon's back. When she felt the distance was achievable, she leaped across the gap and landed on her hands and knees, quickly scrambling to Ameratsu's neck.

*The emperor is dead. An explosion near the palace. I know we're outnumbered and the situation looks grim, but we can't leave the people inside the city to die. Will you help me protect them?*

*Of course I will,* Ameratsu replied. *But first I need to be free of these invisible shackles.*

"Kalea!"

He looked at her, and Lailani pointed down at the enemy.

"The sorcerers are down there. My dragon can't get far unless they die."

Kalea bowed his head. His dragon roared and dived, breathing a fiery torrent among the Roarans. The other dragons descended, adding their fury. Screams filled the air. The soldiers pressed against one another in a frenzied attempt to escape the flames. Their orderly ranks devolved into pandemonium.

*I'm free,* Ameratsu said.

She flew down, sending a stream of her own fire into the Roaran forces. Lailani held on tightly, hiding her face from the heat by burying her head in the crook of her elbow. Ameratsu whipped her tail into a siege tower. The timber snapped and broke in half, the top portion toppling to the ground.

A wave of arrows filled the air, but they weren't from the imperial soldiers. Lailani pressed herself close to Ameratsu as they zipped past. She looked back and saw a rider fall from their dragon, struck by one of the projectiles. A flurry of glowing green energy orbs followed the arrows. They hit both a rider and a dragon. The rider slumped in the saddle, but the dragon screeched in agony and fell from the sky.

Bursts of magic lit up across the Roaran army, and before Lailani's mind could comprehend what was happening, several more dragons were hit. Their numbers dropped in half. Ameratsu soared higher, weaving her body to avoid being struck. Kalea and his dragon joined them, flying side by side while the remaining clan members retreated to the walls.

"We have no defense against their sorcerers," Kalea said. "We need to pull back."

Lailani scanned the army below, looking for Tchi, but the gloom and mass of bodies made it impossible to find the leader. If only they could cut the head from the snake, the body would die.

*Let's get behind the wall,* Lailani said. *We need a plan.*

Ameratsu took them back over the city and they landed outside the palace. Lailani leaped down to the ground and hurried over to Kalea's dragon.

"The gates won't hold forever," she said. "What can we do?"

Kalea joined her on the ground and shook his head. "I don't know. We can't risk being outside the walls, not with their sorcerers taking out our dragons so easily."

"If we could strike the sorcerers down, we would be unstoppable."

"I'm open to ideas," Kalea said.

Lailani didn't have any to offer. She wasn't a leader. She was barely a soldier. The palace doors swung open and Lord Ishida stepped out. He strode over to them and paused.

"Where are the others?"

"Dead, my Lord," Kalea answered. "The Roarans have powerful magic users in their ranks."

"Have they breached the gates?"

"Not yet."

"She is right." Lord Ishida looked at Lailani. "The people are the empire. We must defend them, even if it means we die."

"If we fall, the Roarans will slaughter our people," Lailani said. "Is there no way to get them out of the city?"

"There were tunnels, but the emperor had them filled to keep the Roarans out."

"We could arm the people," Kalea suggested.

Lord Ishida shook his head. "They aren't warriors. They're just as likely to hack their own limbs off as the enemy's. Our only hope is to keep them from getting past the walls."

"Who's in command of the imperial soldiers?" Lailani asked. "Will they flee knowing the emperor is dead?"

"No one knows about his demise," Lord Ishida replied. "We need to keep it that way as long as we can. If the soldiers abandon their posts, we won't have enough men to keep the Roarans at bay."

"We don't have enough men to do that, anyway." Lailani looked from him to Kalea. "I fear this is our final stand against them. What happens here will determine the fate of the empire."

A thunderous crash echoed off the walls around them, and a moment later, a horn blared, followed by shouts and the clash of arms. Lord Ishida drew his sword.

"They've broken through."

ROARAN SOLDIERS POURED into the courtyard. The few imperial soldiers were quickly overrun. Lord Ishida took charge and began issuing orders, rushing forward and cutting down a handful of enemies. Lailani and Kalea drew their blades and joined him. The remaining riders and guards formed into a line beside them, providing an effective defense.

*We can't flame them with you in the way,* Ameratsu said.

*If we give up ground, they'll overtake us. Can you fly behind them and take them out from there?*

The bond filled with Ameratsu's delight and she took to the air, flying over the palace. An orange glow bathed the courtyard as she began breathing fire on the Roarans entering through the damaged portion of the wall. The other dragons followed her example, and with their absence, Lailani felt as though the courtyard was too big to defend.

She kept her thrusts short and controlled, not wanting to overextend herself. A soldier wielding two swords came toward her, his blades weaving in a dangerous pattern. She jabbed the tip of her blade at his left leg, but he deflected the strike with one sword and smacked her weapon with the other, sending it flying from her grasp. Her eyes widened, thinking he had her, but Kalea engaged the man, pulling his attention from her.

Lailani broke from the line and retrieved her sword, then helped Kalea take the dual-wielding Roaran down. They managed to keep the Roarans at bay for a short while, but a few imperial soldiers were cut down and the line crumbled.

"Retreat to the gate!" Lord Ishida roared.

Lailani backtracked as quickly as she could, but she couldn't take her focus off the pressing mob of enemies without risking death. She was on the defensive, slapping attacks away left and right. The gate was closed, and when they reached it, Lailani panicked. They were trapped against the wall.

*We need help,* she told Ameratsu, her eyes scanning the sky. None of the dragons were visible.

*We're fighting our own battle,* the dragon replied. *These sorcerers are wreaking havoc!*

"Get the gates open," Lord Ishida ordered, looking at her.

Lailani turned toward the gates. They were barred closed by a long wooden beam. She sheathed her blade and grabbed one end of the beam and heaved, but it was heavy and she couldn't pull the other end loose. She set it back into place.

"Kalea! I need your help!"

He cut down an enemy and sprinted over, grabbing onto the other end of the beam. Together, they lifted it free of the prongs that held it in place and set it aside.

"Pull back!" Lord Ishida shouted.

Their numbers had dwindled. The situation was grim, and Lailani found herself wondering if staying to defend the city had been the best idea. She pushed the thought away, knowing deep down that what she was doing was the right thing. The other men fled into the city, slamming the gate doors shut behind them.

"There's no way to seal the doors," Kalea said.

"We have to hold them here," Lord Ishida replied.

Lailani drew her sword. There was nowhere to go. She glanced back. The main gate appeared to be holding up against the battering ram. Her attention snapped back to the doors in front of her as the enemy began pushing against them. Lord Ishida and the others pressed their backs against the doors, grunting and straining to keep them closed.

A rumble sounded in the distance, reminding her of thunder. She looked to the sky, praying it wasn't going to rain. Fighting would be difficult enough without being drenched. The sky was clear.

"What is that?" someone shouted.

The noise grew louder as it got closer, and Lailani wondered what sort of weapon the Roarans were bringing against them now. Was it more magic? Or something worse? She kept her eyes upward as she pressed her body against the doors. An enormous shadow passed over them, darting across the city, followed by another. And another.

Flames lit up the sky, and Lailani's eyes widened. They were dragons, but unlike any she'd seen before. They were *winged* dragons. She looked at Kalea. He wore a surprised expression, as did everyone except Lord Ishida. He was smiling.

"Where did they come from?" Kalea asked.

"Osnen," Lord Ishida replied. "The emperor said help was coming, but I never suspected …"

Hope filled her, but they were still in danger until the Roarans were driven back.

*Are you seeing this?*

*I see them,* Ameratsu said. *And they are strong in number.*

*We're saved.*

She couldn't help but wonder what the emperor had bargained in exchange for their help. By all accounts, he'd been a man of pride. Asking for help must have been a blow to his ego, but she was glad he'd humbled himself enough to do so. That small action would ripple across the land. He had saved the empire.

More dragons flew overhead, their fiery breath lighting up the heavens. Magical attacks rained down on the enemy from the riders of Osnen, and a cheer rang out from the soldiers on the wall.

*I'm coming to you,* Ameratsu told her.

Something heavy landed on the other side of the door, and the war song of their enemies turned into terrified screams and gargled death cries. The pressure against the doors let up, and Lailani stepped away, sheathing her blade. The others followed suit, and Lord Ishida pulled the doors open.

Ameratsu stood among a pile of Roaran bodies, the flagstones covered in blood. Those left alive were trapped between her and the other dragons outside the wall. They threw down their weapons and dropped to their knees in surrender.

"Round them up," Lord Ishida ordered Kalea.

The Talon Leader motioned for Lailani and a few others to come with him, and they prodded the Roaran soldiers into moving from the courtyard to the barracks where imperial soldiers promptly shackled them in irons and hauled them off to the dungeon. When they returned to the courtyard, Lailani saw one of the winged dragons had landed near the palace and a man in plate armor was conversing with Lord Ishida. She walked over to where they were and heard part of their conversation.

"That's unfortunate. He made an agreement with my king. I don't suppose you know the details?"

"I'm afraid not."

"Your emperor promised to merge his empire with the Osnen kingdom. There were some things that still needed to be worked out, but if he's dead … I'll have to inform my liege of these events."

"I don't know of this agreement, but if that is what your king has told you, then we are at your mercy."

"You have nothing to fear," the man said. "We are allies, uniting as one. The Roarans have been routed. They flee the battlefield as we speak."

"We are indebted to you for your aid." Lord Ishida offered the man a bow.

Lailani couldn't believe it. The emperor had given up his empire to save his people. Her gaze went to the palace. Perhaps there had been more to him than she knew. The man from Osnen climbed onto his dragon and took to the sky. She thought dragons looked odd with wings, but the Osnen soldiers probably thought the same about the Terran dragons. Lord Ishida looked at her.

"What you did was very honorable," he said. "Your father will be proud when he learns of your deeds."

"I don't know about that. His dragon is dead because of my actions. I wouldn't be surprised if he never forgives me."

Lord Ishida's face tightened, but he said nothing. She assumed he felt guilty about executing Daigo, but was too proud to admit it. She didn't need his apology. It wouldn't bring the dragon back, and it wouldn't make her feel any better.

"What will you do now?" she asked, changing the subject.

"I will serve whoever is to rule next. It is my duty. And you?"

She nodded, expecting as much. "I will go home. I miss my father, and there is much that I must tell him."

"I rescind my banishment," he said. "If you find that the simple life doesn't suit you anymore, you are welcome to return to my command. I can always use men like you ..." He paused, realizing his error. "The empire could benefit from those with bravery such as yours. I will speak to the king about the laws in place. Perhaps he will be less inclined to prohibit women from positions of power."

"Perhaps he will," Lailani agreed.

They stood in silence for a moment, then Lailani bowed to Lord Ishida and left, walking to where Ameratsu was. She climbed up the dragon's shoulder and seated herself in place. Kalea strode over, lifting his arm to catch her attention.

"I assume you're going home?"

"I am."

"Tell my father I'm all right, would you?"

Lailani nodded. "I will."

Kalea stared at her, something in his eyes that she'd never noticed before, but she didn't know what it was.

"I'll see you again," he said.

"I hope so."

Kalea backed away and Ameratsu leaped into the air.

*Do you know where the Perched Cay is?*

*Yes.*

*Take me there, please.*

30

THE SUN WAS cresting on the horizon as Lailani stood outside her home. The islanders would wake to start their work soon. She had faced many things over the last few days, but facing her father now was the most frightening of them all.

Would he be disappointed with her, or would he disown her completely? Daigo was dead, and it was all her fault. That alone was enough justification for her father to never wish to see her again. There was also the fact that she had run off with his armor and sword, both of which were in her bag.

Lailani took a deep breath and opened the door. She stepped inside and saw her father sitting at the table. He looked up at her. The silence stretched between them.

"Father," she finally said.

"Lailani." He rose from his chair. "Do I see a ghost before me?"

"No, it's really me."

Hayate shuffled over to her, his frame bent from the disease that had consumed him. He opened his arms and she embraced him, holding him tight. Her emotions took control, and she wept. Hayate said nothing. He just held her, comforting her as only a father could. When she calmed herself, she released him and stepped back.

"Forgive me, father."

She told him about everything. Her plot, about Daigo and Huou, and the men she slaughtered at the Roaran camp. He listened stoically and let her spill her heart, and when she was done, he hugged her.

"You have seen more in a few weeks than many will their entire lives. The internal strength you have shown certainly comes from your mother. She would be proud of you. I am honored to call you my daughter, Lailani."

"You aren't angry with me? Daigo would still be alive if—"

Hayate raised his hand, interrupting her. "His loss is a powerful blow to me, but I lost him long ago. I closed my end of the bond when your mother died because I didn't want to cast my grief on him. As the days passed, I kept the bond sealed shut because I could not stand to feel the loss of another."

"Dragons live much longer than we do," Lailani said.

"I know, but grief can give you illogical fears. Those fears took hold of my mind. I told myself I would be free if I died in battle against the Roarans, and I was ready for my life to end. When I woke and found you were gone, I went to Daigo's cave and found he was missing as well. When you didn't return by nightfall, I knew what you had done."

Lailani never knew her father struggled that deeply over her mother's death. He had been sad, but she thought he recovered well from it. How wrong she had been. Hayate sighed.

"I need to sit down. My bones ache when I stand too long." He returned to his chair. "I was angry with you at first. I felt as though you had stolen my rightful death. As the thought of you dying dwelled in my mind, I realized I was a fool. My fear of losing Daigo ruled my life, and I never considered that I might lose you. My anger drained from me then, as well as my fears."

"Did you feel it? When Daigo died?"

"Yes." Hayate's eyes became glossy with tears. "Even though I kept the bond closed all these years, the pain of his death pushed through all my defenses. I feel it even now."

"I'm sorry," Lailani said again.

"I forgive you. What you did was dangerous and foolish, but there is nothing more honorable than to lie down your life for another."

"Will I ever stop seeing their faces?" she asked. "Of the men I killed?"

"I don't know."

"Do you remember those you have killed?"

"Yes."

Lailani nodded. The images of their faces were like a brand on her mind. Perhaps it would be a good thing if she never forgot them.

"I need to tell Huou's family."

"It will be hard on them, but it will comfort them to know that he died fighting for them."

She knew her father was right, but the words felt hollow to her. Huou had been her friend since childhood, and the world felt a little darker without his presence. She still had Kalea, and now she had Ameratsu. The dragon flooded the bond with comfort, feeling her sadness.

Lailani waited until she felt strong enough to face Huou's family to see them. After delivering the news and feeling her heart wrench again at their reactions, she went to the beach where Daigo's cave was. Ameratsu was there, curled up on the sand, basking under the sun.

She joined the dragon and watched the waves lap at the shore, breathing in the sea-scented air. The Roarans were defeated and the empire was changing, hopefully for the better. Only time would tell. Lailani sat down and lounged beside Ameratsu, closing her eyes against the sun.

Her life would never be the same.

## THE END

# PRONUNCIATION GUIDE

*Characters*
Lailani – Lay-Lah-Nee
Daigo – Day-Go
Kalea – Kuh-Lay-Uh
Mukani – Muh-Kahn-ee
Hayate – h-ae-Y-AE-t-ai
Huou – He-yow
Ishida – Ish-ee-duh
Katsuo – Kaat-soo-ow
Ameratsu – Ahm-er-aht-sue
Tchi – Chee

*Surname*
Seijin – Say-gin

*Locations*
Terran – Tear-uhn
Shojin – Show-gin
Shingtai – Shing-tie
Mu River – Mew

*People*
Roaran – Roar-an
Terranese – Tear-uhn-ease

# ACKNOWLEGEMENTS

I want to thank all of the Kickstarter backers for making the paperback and hardback versions of this book for happening. It wouldn't have been possible without you all.

List names here.

# DEAR READER

Thank you for reading my book. It was an absolute joy telling this story, and I hope that my love of Asian culture poured through to you. I spent time as a child in Okinawa, Japan and have always had a deep appreciation for everything I experienced there.

I hope you enjoyed it!

# ABOUT THE AUTHOR

Hey there!

I write fantasy and space opera, and you can find all my books in many different ebook stores. You can check out my website for more information about my books, my next projects, and events I'll be attending.

If you enjoyed this book, I'd love your feedback in the form of a review on Amazon or Goodreads.

Thanks for reading!

-Richard

Website: www.richardfierce.com

Facebook: www.facebook.com/dragonfirepress

TikTok: www.tiktok.com/TTPdSrPTBx